CROSS FIRE

"Well, the elusive Mr. Morgan. So good of you to let us know where you were. I want those papers now. Hand them over and we'll forget I ever saw you."

"What papers, Mr. O'Gallon?"

"No time for games, Morgan. I'll start shooting you in the knees and work up to your crotch until you tell me where they are."

Morgan raised his brows. It was time. Now! He dove toward the floor drawing iron as he went down. Two shots thundered in the back room of the Miller General Store. One hit Morgan in the chest and hurried his dive to the floor.

He wasn't sure where the other shot went. For a moment a black cloud hovered over him. Then everything faded away....

The *Buckskin* Series:

1: RIFLE RIVER
2: GUNSTOCK
3: PISTOLTOWN
4: COLT CREEK
5: GUNSIGHT GAP
6: TRIGGER SPRING
7: CARTRIDGE COAST
8: HANGFIRE HILL
9: CROSSFIRE COUNTRY
#10: BOLT ACTION
#11: TRIGGER GUARD
#12: RECOIL
#13: GUNPOINT
#14: LEVER ACTION
#15: SCATTERGUN
#16: WINCHESTER VALLEY
#17: GUNSMOKE GORGE
#18: REMINGTON RIDGE
#19: SHOTGUN STATION
#20: PISTOL GRIP
#21: PEACEMAKER PASS
#22: SILVER CITY CARBINE
#23: CALIFORNIA CROSSFIRE
#24: COLT CROSSING
#25: POWDER CHARGE
#26: LARAMIE SHOWDOWN
#27: DOUBLE ACTION
#28: APACHE RIFLES
#29: RETURN FIRE
#30: RIMFIRE REVENGE
#31: TOMBSTONE TEN GAUGE

DEATH DRAW

32

BUCKSKIN

KIT DALTON

LEISURE BOOKS NEW YORK CITY

A LEISURE BOOK®

May 1992

Published by

Dorchester Publishing Co., Inc.
276 Fifth Avenue
New York, NY 10001

Printed in the United States of America.

Chapter One

Lee Buckskin Morgan squinted to be sure he saw what he thought he did through the shimmering heat waves. Nothing looked right around Old Charley's cabin in the high country 20 miles north of Denver. He had dismounted under the cover of some brush and had walked up to where he could better see the place.

No smoke came from the chimney.

Old Charley's jackass wasn't in the tumble-down pole corral next to the cabin.

Howlin' Mad, Old Charley's mongrel, wasn't stretched out on the rough wooden porch in back or feverishly barking at a crow.

Morgan checked his six-gun. The Colt .45 lay in its leather holster, loaded and ready. The bang of a screen door brought his head up in an instant, the iron in his strong right hand as he stared at the back door.

His mouth fell open in amazement. A small child walked to the edge of the porch and sat down. He was too far away to tell how old the child was or if it were a boy or a girl.

Morgan circled the cabin staying out of sight in the brush until he made it to the rear of the cabin where there were no windows. He charged the 50 yards to the side of the rough logs and panted a moment, catching his breath. He was out of shape. That's what good living in Denver for two weeks did to a man.

He slid to the end of the logs and looked around at the back porch. He hadn't heard a sound from the cabin, but through the eight inch logs, that wasn't unusual.

The child still sat on the back porch. It was a little girl of about four, tears had made muddy tracks down her face. Her hair was long, blonde and looked as if it hadn't been combed for days.

When he whistled like a meadowlark, the girl turned and her eyes went wide as she stared at him. Then she jumped off the porch and ran to him with her arms wide.

"Daddy?" she asked in a small voice filled with pain and anger and even some fear.

Buckskin knelt in the red soil, caught the small girl in his arms and held her.

"Are you my daddy?" the winsome voice asked again.

"No, I'm afraid not. Is your mommie here?"

The small blonde head nodded without leaving the comfort of his shoulder.

"Is there anyone else here?"

This time her head shook for a no. Buckskin felt considerably relieved. He was worried when Old Charley's place looked so deserted. The old man could have gone to town for supplies.

Morgan stood and carried the small bundle through the back door of Old Charley's cabin. It looked about the same. Two rooms. Some dirty pots on the small iron stove. Fireplace cold. The small girl motioned.

"Mommie's in there," she said pointing to the second room beyond the partition of pine logs. "My mommie is sick."

Still carrying the girl, he looked in the room and found a young woman lying on Old Charley's bunk bed. Her eyes were closed. When the girl wiggled and he let her down, she ran to the bed and touched the woman's shoulder.

"Mommie. Mommie. A man's here."

The woman's eyes snapped open, and a frown covered her face. When she reached for something beside her, he saw it was a six-gun.

"No need for the weapon, ma'am," Morgan said gently. "I won't do you no harm."

She watched him from soft green eyes. Her hair was unkempt, her face pale and drawn. Then he saw the bloody spot on her side, just below her breast.

"Ma'am, looks like you're hurt."

She shook her head. "No sir, not hurt. I'm near dead. No chance I can get through this." She gasped, and her eyes shut as pain drilled through her. A soft cry of anger and defeat seeped from her lips, but she fought it down.

"Promise me you'll take care of little Lisa. She's all I have left. Promise!" Her voice rose.

"Yes, ma'am. I'll see that she gets to town and to some good folks. Don't worry about that. I'll look at that gunshot wound and have you better in no time."

He bent to look at the wound, but she shook her head gently.

"Don't bother none. I'm most gone. Been here three days. He just rode off and left us." She motioned to a small jerry-built table next to the bed. "That package. Promise me you'll take it to where it goes." She gasped, and her face writhed with the pain. A moment later she opened her eyes and stared at him. "Take the package to Wang Fan Too in Santa Fe. He'll know what to do." She coughed and blood surged into her mouth and seeped from her lips. She shivered, and her eyes glazed over for a moment.

"Promise," she said with a force he couldn't imagine that she had strength left to generate.

"Yes, ma'am, I'll get it there. Who shot you?"

"Man I trusted. He wanted the package. Lisa here hid it from him. She's a good hider. I'm not feeling so good."

He tried to look at the bullet hole again, but she pushed his hands away. "Take care of my baby and find the man who killed me." She lifted her hand off the thin blouse she wore, then it dropped. Her head rolled gently to the side facing him, and her eyes stared through him into eternity.

Morgan took a deep breath, picked up Lisa and carried her outside into the mountain sunshine.

"Is Mommie still sick?"

"Not any more, Lisa."

"Did Mommie go away? She said she had to go away and leave me."

"Yes, she went away. Shouldn't you be having a nap about now? Let me fix you a blanket under that tree over there. Later on we'll ride into town."

"Mommie won't be coming?"

"No, she's already gone away, like she told you."

When Lisa slept, Morgan would dig a shallow grave. He looked for some soft ground and found it near the creek. He also found another grave with a sawed marker and with Old Charley's name on it. From the pencil lettering on the marker, Old Charley died a month ago.

Morgan began to dig. Lee Buckskin Morgan was 28 years-old and stood an even six feet tall. He weighed in at 185 pounds and was trim and in good physical condition. Usually he was clean-shaven with brown eyes, brownish blonde hair, a strong mouth and a square chin. He wore a high-crowned brown Stetson with a black headband with red diamonds on it.

By trade he was a detective, working for himself and as the spirit moved him. Right now he was on his way to Cheyenne and the railroad back east where there was an offer of a job.

Morgan was sweating before he finished the four foot deep grave.

By the time Lisa woke up, Morgan had wrapped the woman in a blanket and buried her.

Inside the cabin he found two battered carpetbags. The woman's contained clothes, a family Bible, a writing pad and pencils. According to the family Bible, the woman's name was Bernice Upton. The only place named in the Bible was some town in Illinois. Lisa was four, and her birthday was in December.

He put the Bible and pad and pencils in the smaller carpetbag with Lisa's few clothes and went outside.

It took him half an hour to find the tracks. They were two, maybe three days old. One horse had a rider, the other was on a lead line. They angled south toward Denver.

It was still before noon. Morgan checked the larder and found a can of beans, some weevil laden flour and a tin of syrup. He heated the beans, broke out the half a loaf of bread he had bought at the last town and brought Lisa in for their meal. He made coffee and gave Lisa water from the stream.

"Mommie went away?" she asked when she looked at the empty bed.

"Yes, she told you she would."

An hour later they moved along the scratchy trail to the south. The rider had been in no rush. Morgan kept to the trail and seven miles later they came into the village of Lafayette. The small girl had sat on the saddle in front of him all the way with never a complaint.

As they came into the town, she turned and watched him. "Are you going to be my new daddy?"

Buckskin's heart turned over, and he had to take a moment before he could answer. He'd never come up against a problem quite like this before. No, not a problem—a situation. She was a precious little jewel, but he had no way to care for her. Besides he had a killer to find and a package to deliver.

He went into the Miller General Store. There were about 20 stores and saloons in the settlement and maybe five times that many houses. He had no idea why a town had sprung up here.

A woman behind the counter was thick-waisted with beefy arms and a small cherubic face. Bright blue eyes danced as she looked at the small traveler. She waved at Lisa, and her smile lit up the whole store.

"Well, young lady, this must be your first trip to town. I haven't seen you before."

"My mommie went away. This is my new daddy."

The merchant lady looked at Morgan, and a flicker of raw passion brought a movement to her shoulders that jiggled her breasts.

"Trouble in the family?" she asked.

"More than a little," Morgan said. He picked a piece of horehound candy from a jar on the counter, and gave Lisa the treat. "Look around and see if you can find something pretty," Morgan said with a gentleness that was new and strange to him. He'd known this little girl for five hours and already she was changing his life.

When she skipped down the aisle between axes and teakettles and pots and pans, Morgan turned to the woman.

"I found her ma shot about seven or eight miles out in Old Charley's cabin. She died before she said much."

"Bet that upset Old Charley. Old cuss ain't been in for a spell."

"Old Charley wasn't there, and I found a grave marker with a month-old date on it. Could be his last resting spot. What I'm wondering is if you saw a man riding into town leading a horse last two or three days?"

"A dozen maybe. What this one look like?"

"I don't know. Lisa told me he was big and had a gun. Not a lot of help."

"This little Lisa is an orphan, then?"

"Far as I can tell. Her ma asked me to take care of the sprout, but I'm a traveling man. I can't much take proper care of a little girl like Lisa."

"Damn straight there," the woman said. She held out a sturdy hand. "Donna Miller. I run this place. My husband died three years ago. I'm doing good with the store. My bet would be you're looking for a home for this little darling."

"About the read on it."

"You also trying to find the killer?"

"Promised the little mother."

"God-awful hard job. Two or three days ago. Could have been anybody, and he might be two or three days down the trail past Denver or lost in that dirty town."

"True. What about Lisa?"

"Mrs. Larson might be kindly to the idea of taking her on. She lost a two year-old to the fever a month ago. Only youngun' they had. I might talk to her, if'n it's all right. This tad have a last name?"

"Upton, Lisa Upton."

The woman behind the counter sucked in a breath. "We had some Uptons here a year ago. Was the mother's name Bernice?"

Morgan nodded. "Family Bible says it was."

The woman came from behind the counter, her face full of emotion. He wasn't sure if it was fear or anger. "Don't use the name Upton around town. Still lots of bad blood here. Seems like she might have been trying to get home. Only her folks left a year ago. I'm also postmistress here. I kind of keep track of people.

"Bernice married a man her father hated. They ran off six years ago. Went to Denver, then on to Santa Fe down in New Mexico Territory. I kind of lost track then."

"What's the bad blood about, just that?"

Mrs. Miller shook her head. "That's just the start of it." She looked up at Morgan. "Can you take care of yourself? By the way that gun is tied low, I'd say you can use your iron."

Morgan nodded. "I can shoot some."

"Don't use the name Upton around town. You might get some handbills printed and tack them up. Something like 'Found one small girl and valuables North of town. Anyone interested come to some saloon at four o'clock today.'"

Morgan scowled. "Then you think the man who shot Bernice is still in town?"

"He'd stay here and wait for orders. A lot more involved in this than the death of Bernice or the welfare of her darling little girl. I might just keep her myself. Gets lonely around the house. My two younguns are grown and gone."

"Where's the printer?"

An hour later, Morgan had the flyers printed. He borrowed some tacks and a hammer from Mrs. Miller and put up 20 posters around town on buildings and fences. It was then nearly two o'clock. He had named the Beer Barrel Saloon as the meeting place but he didn't bother telling the owner about it.

Mrs. Miller had taken Lisa in hand. She gave her a sponge bath between customers, outfitted her with new clothes from her stock and fixed her a proper meal. Then Lisa took an afternoon nap in the living quarters above the store.

Morgan sat on the steps outside the general store and watched the posters. The first dozen men and women who read them simply moved on. One man read the notice, stopped and frowned, then read it again. He ripped it off the wall of the barber shop and hurried with it down the street.

Morgan was 50 feet behind him. He turned in at a stairway that went to the second floor of a building over a saloon and a hardware store.

Morgan went up the steps slowly. At the top he saw three doors opening off a hallway. The man was gone. One door said: "J. Burel Halstead, Lawyer." The second door was unmarked, and the third read: "Gunther Johnson, Land Office, Real Estate, Investments."

Morgan eased back down the steps and took up his post again. Two dozen more people stopped and read the notice but were not affected. Then a small man wearing a suit and a derby hat read the poster and sauntered away.

Something in his attitude caught Morgan's attention, so he followed the man. The small fashion plate paused near the same steps leading up to where Morgan had been before. When the dapper dan thought no one was watching him, he slipped up the steps and out of sight.

Back at the general store, Morgan waited until Mrs. Miller was finished with a customer.

"I'm interested in two men, Halstead and Johnson. Would they have anything to do with this problem that Bernice Upton had?"

Mrs. Miller stared at him in amazement. "How on earth did you come up with those two names so quickly?"

Morgan told her.

"Halstead is the rotten heart of this town. He's a lawyer and a good one. He's cheated, swindled and taken advantage of half the folks in Lafayette. Oh, all legally, of course. Gunther Johnson is the other half of the coin. He owns the rest of the land in town. Not all of his moves were legal, but as soon as anyone challenged him, the man wound up dead or run out of town."

Morgan frowned. "How do they tie in with Santa Fe, New Mexico Territory?"

"I don't know. Not even sure that I want to know."

Lisa ran up, and Morgan saw she now wore a different dress than she had on before. She hugged Mrs. Miller's sturdy leg and looked up past the skirts.

"You have a cookie?" Lisa asked.

Donna Miller melted. Her stern expression came apart as she scooped up the child and hugged her, then she stepped over to the cookie jar and took out two. They were homemade from Mrs. Miller's own oven.

"What do you say?" the shopkeeper asked.

"Thank you, Mrs. Miller," Lisa said. She sat down on the floor cross-legged and took the first bite out of one of the cookies.

"I don't know nothing about Santa Fe." Mrs. Miller said.

Morgan snorted. "Which means to me that you do know and wished you didn't, but you won't tell me about it. Will I get killed finding out?"

"You could. More than one man's been killed in this scheme."

"If you send me in blind, I'll have to take Lisa along. They won't blow a man away with a shotgun when he's carrying a little girl like her."

Mrs. Miller took her turn scowling. She shook her head. "No, no, you can't do that. Let me keep her here. If anything happens, I'll raise her as my own. Nobody will know who she is but you and me."

Morgan felt a flood of relief to be no longer responsible for the little girl. He nodded. "All right, you can keep her. But you have to tell me all you know about this before I meet whoever they send to the saloon at four o'clock. We have twenty minutes."

Chapter Two

Mrs. Miller stared hard at Morgan, frowned for a second, then shrugged.

"Guess I wouldn't feel right if you went over there and got yourself gunned down. Best you know as much as I do. What I'm going to tell you could get us both killed if they find out we are on to them. Don't ever let anything I tell you be known that it came from me. Agreed?"

Morgan nodded.

A chiming clock struck a quarter to the hour, and Morgan pointed to it.

"Yes. Time. What Mr. Upton didn't have I reckon. He worked with Gunther Johnson. I never knew what he did for the man, but it was out of town somewhere. Spent a lot of time there and then toward September of that year he came back. I saw them together around town.

"Then it seemed the two had a falling out,

and Mr. Upton said some things around town about Mr. Johnson that the rich man didn't like. Next thing I know the Uptons are gone, nobody knows where they went and nobody gave me a new address for them.

"About a month later a letter comes from Mrs. Upton asking any mail to be forwarded to a store in Santa Fe."

"What was the name of the store?"

"That I still remember. It was the Wang Fan Too General Store in Santa Fe. So I forwarded all I had and one or two pieces that came in after that."

"That's all you know?"

"In this town, that's enough to get yourself killed. Gunther Johnson came in asking if I had a forwarding address for Upton. That was about a week after I had received it. He said he had wages due to send him, but he wasn't sure of his new address.

"I saw the look in that man's eyes, and I lied. Said I didn't have no new address. That's easier than explaining that I can't give out the new address. Post Office regulations."

"Yes, ma'am. How does this Burel Halstead fit in?"

"The good Lord only knows. He's owned by Johnson. Does all of his legal work and land grabbing. Whatever he knows, Johnson soon knows. Not much backbone, that one, but he's hooked up with the richest man in town."

"This isn't much for me to go on, Mrs. Miller."

"Best I can do. Didn't say I knew much. How you aim to find the killer?"

"Not sure. First, I'll see who shows up at the saloon looking for me."

"Could be a couple of fast guns," Mrs. Miller said as she tossed him a cookie from the barrel.

"True, but I've got ways of discouraging that." Morgan checked the clock. "I better get moving." He munched on the oatmeal cookie on his way to his horse at the front of the store. He took two items out of his saddlebags and pushed them into his rear pocket.

The Beer Barrel Saloon was only half a block away. He quickly went in and right to the bar. The bartender looked up and Morgan waved him down to the near end of the polished surface.

"I tacked up a notice for somebody looking for me to come in here," Morgan said. "Figured you could use the business. If anybody asks about the guy who found one small girl and valuables north of town, tell them I'll be in the alley out back."

Morgan slid the man a silver dollar. "Be obliged if you could tell that to anybody who asks."

The barkeep made the silver dollar vanish in an instant and grinned.

"Yes, sir. No problem with me. I can give a message like that long as need be. The back door to the alley is right over there. Outhouse back there, too, so it gets some traffic."

Morgan nodded and walked out to the alley. There were half a dozen other buildings that backed up to the alley, but there were open spaces as well between the buildings to the left.

To the right was another building that was longer and went back almost to the edge of the alley. On the side of the building was a jumble of planks and boards leaning against the wall. Morgan found plenty of room to push in behind the two-inch thick planks and still be able to see the back door of the saloon. The heavy wood would stop a rifle bullet.

He leaned against the building behind the planks and waited.

Less than a minute later, a man came out the back of the saloon and headed for the outhouse. He returned a few moments later to the saloon.

Then two men came out of the door and looked around.

"Hey, where are you? Somebody back here the one who found that little girl and some belongings of hers?"

Morgan studied the pair. Both had six-guns tied low, and both looked like they could use their iron. They were messengers with a story of quick death.

Morgan fisted his own Colt and edged it around a plank so he had an open field of fire.

"Lace your hands on top of your head and step this way," Morgan boomed at the two strangers. They turned toward where his voice came from. One started lifting his hands, but the other snorted.

"No way I'm letting my hands be that far from my iron."

"You want to die with that in mind?" Morgan barked. He fired a round between the man's boots.

"Easy!"

"Lift them and walk this way," Morgan called. Both men did as instructed. When they were within ten feet of the planks, Morgan told them to stop.

"Now, what do you know about a small blonde girl and her possessions that I found north of town?"

Both men remained silent.

"Will a slug in your knee help you remember? One shot there and you'll be crippled for life."

"No, damnit, don't shoot me!" the shorter man yelled.

"Shut up, you fool!" the other one snapped.

Morgan shot him in the thigh, missing the bone. He went down screaming.

"Move for your iron and you're dead," Morgan said. He stepped out from behind the planks. The moment he did, a revolver roared twice from the door of the saloon 40 feet away. Both rounds missed.

Morgan returned two shots, then dodged behind the planks again. When the saloon door slammed shut, the man in the dirt screamed for someone to help him.

"Tell me who sent you, who hired you to gun me down," Morgan barked.

The smaller man with his hands still on his head blinked and nodded. "O.K. Man was Rocky Paulson."

"Who does he work for?"

"For Mr. Johnson. Everybody knows that."

"He a gunman?"

"Yes sir."

"Shut up, stupid. Rocky won't like it."

"Leastwise I didn't get shot," the shorter man said.

"Where can I find Rocky?"

"In the Dirty Dozen Saloon, down the street," the shorter man said. "Can we leave now?"

"Yeah, get out of here and take your bleeding partner with you."

Morgan watched the two struggle down the alley to the cross street. When they were gone, he left the planks and sprinted past the end of the building and out of sight of the back door of the saloon.

He went through to the street where a building had burned down and looked for the Dirty Dozen Saloon on the main avenue. He should have found out what Rocky looked like. Another silver dollar would do the trick.

The Dirty Dozen Saloon was a step down from the previous one. It was a barrel bar, with two barrels on end with planks over them to serve as the bar. A bench had been built in along the wall for sitting, and there were only three tables for card games. All the tables were busy.

Morgan bought a beer for a dime and asked the barkeep where he could find Rocky. The bartender glared at him from one good eye and one glass one that didn't move.

"If you don't know him, you ain't supposed to find him," he said.

Morgan grabbed the bartender by the shirt front and pulled him forward off his feet so he leaned on the side of the bar.

"Look, idiot, you want me to smash in your face or put a bullet through your mouth? If Rocky is here point him out to me, otherwise get set to die."

The words were steady, and deadly, so soft that no one else in the saloon could hear them. The man's eyes went wide, and he nodded toward the back of the room.

"Last table, gent with the gray hat."

"That's better. Now keep quiet and don't signal him, or I'll be back." Morgan walked along the bar, then casually back to the last table. He saw the rear door a few feet behind the four poker players.

Morgan worked around until he was directly behind the man the barkeep had pointed out. He looked at the man's cards as he fanned them quickly, then closed them.

"Twenty dollars," Rocky said.

Morgan moved quickly, wrapping his left forearm around Rocky's chin and pressing it against his throat. At the same time, Morgan's .45 rested on Rocky's shoulder so he could see the muzzle.

"Easy, nice and easy. Stand up and move with me, or you're a corpse looking for a pine box."

Rocky grunted, and Morgan lessened the pressure on his throat so he could breathe.

He stood, and Morgan walked him backwards toward the door. He kicked it open and edged through, then spun Rocky around and pinned him against the now shut saloon door.

"Your name Rocky Paulson?"

The man struggled, gasping to get his breath.

"Yeah." It came out a wheeze.

"Why did Johnson want me dead because of some little blonde girl?"

"Don't know why."

Morgan checked over the man. He was about five-eight, dark hair, clean-shaven except for a handlebar moustache. There was a two-inch scar on his right cheek. His dark eyes were filled with hate.

"Any reason I shouldn't gun you dead right here, Rocky?"

"Yeah. I don't know who you are."

"I'm the gent you sent two gunsharps to kill. They didn't quite make it."

Rocky began to shake. "Not my doing. Johnson told me to take care of you. He saw your notice.

Somebody brought it to him. He figured who it had to be."

"You killed the little girl's mother?"

"No!" His eyes flared. "I wasn't even out there. Somebody else Johnson hired went after them. Said he got drunk and shot the woman, figured she was dead. Then the little girl ran off in some trees and hid. He was so drunk he couldn't find her so he took off figuring she couldn't make it on her own."

"What's this spot's name?"

"Don't know."

Morgan brought the side of the heavy .45 down across Rocky's face. The blow brought blood across his cheek and forehead and drove him to the ground, wedged against the door.

"Oh, God! I'm bleeding!"

"Just the start of your bleeding. I asked you who killed the little girl's mother."

"Brice O'Gallon. Little bit of a guy no more than five feet tall, but mean as sin and twice as crooked."

"Where is he now?"

"Gone. Johnson sent him away somewhere."

"Maybe it's time I had a talk with this Mr. Johnson."

"Hard man to get to see," Rocky said.

A rifle erupted from the mouth of the alley 50 yards away, and the hot slug burned a crease across Morgan's upper left arm. He spun away, dove to the side and came up behind some wooden whiskey boxes. Two rifle slugs drove into the wood, splintering it but missing Morgan. He rolled again against the side of the building next door so he was out of the line of fire from down the alley.

He eased upward and saw that Rocky was gone. A second later two six-guns fired at him from the partly opened door, and Morgan did another dive and roll. He came to his feet running and darted across the alley.

A shot from the rifle missed, and in a few seconds he was out of range of the six-guns at the door. He turned and put a round into the saloon's rear wall and heard the door slam shut.

Morgan ran through the empty lot to the street behind Main, then down to the cross street. He refilled his six shooter as he ran, charging all six chambers.

Mrs. Miller hadn't been exaggerating. Just because he said he found a small blonde girl north of town at least five people had tried to kill him. What was going on in this town? At least he had a name of the killer, Brice O'Gallon. If he was working for Johnson, he'd show up here sooner or later.

Morgan found the back door of the general store and slipped inside when no one was looking. Mrs. Miller seemed relieved to see him.

He told her what happened.

She lifted her brows and furnished little Lisa with a pad and a pencil to play with. "So, now you've met some of our town's leading gunmen. Not a friendly place right now. I told you that Johnson was a tough nut."

"What does he look like and where does he live?"

"Johnson is not a man about town. He seldom leaves his office and living quarters over the hardware. Good reason. I haven't seen him in two or three years. I'd say he weighs at least four hundred pounds. He's maybe five feet six, so that makes him almost square."

"He controls everything from upstairs?"

"Yes, and with the men he hires. He came to town with some inherited money fifteen years ago and has taken charge of everything he could get his hands on. Only the last five years or so he's grown so huge."

Morgan shook his head. "If he has all of this, what more does he want?"

"Power. He's the kind of man who feeds on power. The more he has, the more he wants. He'd like to be Territorial Governor. Right now his brother-in-law has that job. Came out appointed from Washington."

"How do I get in to see him? Does he have guards?"

Mrs. Miller laughed. "He owns the town. He has half a dozen men guarding the front and rear entrance to his building. There are no other buildings with access to his. He lives in a fort up there. That front office is just window dressing. He's never in there. That's the first guard's job, watching that office and the door."

"What's his weak point? Every man has a spot where he can be attacked. What's Johnson's?"

"His main vice is eating and drinking. He sends a light wagon to Denver every morning to meet the first stage out of Cheyenne. It meets the train and picks up all sorts of exotic fruits and vegetables he orders from New York. He gets clams and lobster from Maine in boxes filled with ice. He's a food nut."

Lisa finished a picture and showed it to Morgan. He grinned, forgetting his mission. The picture was little more than wavy lines in bold reds and greens.

"What a pretty picture, Lisa," Morgan said. She sat on his lap and showed him how she made it and what each line meant. Mrs. Miller smiled.

"I see your weakness, hard-bitten gunsharp. Little girls will do you in every time."

Morgan nodded. "This is something new for me. Never been around little ones like Lisa before."

"Won't help you with Johnson. He hates kids. He does love beer and wine, however. Didn't like the taste of the local brewery beer, so he bought the plant, hired a brewmaster from Germany and now has the best beer in the whole of Colorado."

Morgan put Lisa back with her drawing and paced the counter area of the store. When Mrs. Miller came back from waiting on a customer he had a new question for her.

"What about Johnson and women?"

"He loves them. Three at a time from what I've heard. But then he owns the three biggest saloons in town so he has his choice of the working girls from upstairs at the saloons."

"So that's out. I'm trying to figure the best way to get to this man. He must have a weak point somewhere."

"I never have thought of one." She paused a moment. "Look, maybe you should get a hotel room and we'll talk about this tomorrow." Mrs. Miller frowned. "Why you want to tangle with him anyway? You said the man who killed Bernice Upton was sent out of town."

Morgan nodded and picked out a piece of the horehound candy. "He was, but Johnson gave the order to kill her, so he's just as guilty as the man who pulled the trigger. I want them both."

"Why? You just stumbled on this whole thing."

"True, but sometimes something just feels right, the way this does. Besides, I promised the little lady I'd do some favors for her. One of them was take care of little Lisa. From the looks of things, she'll never get out of your clutches."

Mrs. Miller only smiled, caught Lisa and hugged her. Lisa hugged her back.

Morgan grinned. "Looks like I've got the first part of the promise taken care of. Now, I think it's time I find a hotel and get some rest in a real bed for a change."

Chapter Three

Morgan moved his horse to a livery, then took a room at the Princess, the only hotel in town. It had a small dining room, and he decided to eat there rather than try to find a better restaurant. He had nearly finished the roast beef, potatoes, gravy and three vegetables when a woman walked in and looked around. There were only eight people in the room since the place was about to close.

She saw Morgan and came his way. He knew she was trouble the moment he saw her, but she was the kind of trouble he didn't mind once in a while. She had an easy way of walking that made her glide across the room, hips working smoothly under her long skirt.

She was tall and had long blonde hair and a pretty face that made him watch her all the way across the room. She stopped beside him. Blue eyes stared down at him, then she crinkled her eyes into a small frown.

"I wonder if you could help me," she said. Her voice came softly, a little lower than he figured it would be, and it gave her a breathy, interesting sound.

Morgan started to stand up, but she touched his shoulder and slid into the chair beside him.

When she sat down the white blouse swept forward, revealing a line of cleavage between her breasts. A moment later it fell back in place.

"How could I help you?" Morgan asked.

"I lost my room key and the clerk is being mean, telling me I have to pay a dollar for a new one, and I don't have another dollar to spare. Could you talk to him for me?"

Morgan was through with his supper, so he pushed back and stood up. The woman came to her feet as well. She was a little taller than he had figured, maybe five-seven.

"I'd be glad to talk to the room clerk, Miss . . ."

"Oh, my name is Kristen, and my room is on the second floor. I don't know how I can thank you."

As he let her walk ahead, he could see a hint of how well her hips worked under the fabric of her dress. At the clerk's window, Morgan turned on a heavy scowl and called to the young man behind the desk.

"I understand this lady needs a key to her room and you won't give her a spare. That's no way to run a hotel. Is the night manager here?"

"No. We don't have a night manager."

"I'd appreciate your giving the lady a key to her room, otherwise I'll have to come behind your small desk here, take it apart, do some serious

damage to your face and find that key by myself.
Do we understand each other?"

The young man turned into jelly. He licked his
lips, and one hand darted under the counter and
brought up a key.

"I just found one," he said lamely.

Kristen snatched it out of his hand and marched
toward the stairs. She was halfway there before
she turned to see if Morgan followed her. He
had not moved. She motioned with her head
for him to come, and when she was well up
the steps he followed. He knew she was trouble, but he was curious exactly what kind of
trouble.

He remembered what Mrs. Miller had said
about people "disappearing". Not a bloody shoot-
out on Main Street, rather a quiet kill somewhere
and the body disposed of neatly.

By the time he was at the top of the steps, he
found her waiting for him just down the hall. She
had the door to 212 open and stood there.

When Morgan walked up, he saw that she had
unbuttoned two of the fasteners on her blouse.

"Could you come in a minute? I want to thank
you for helping me. I don't know what I would
have done without your talking to that desk clerk."
Her lower lip even quivered.

He nodded, and she stepped into the room. As
soon as she moved, he pulled his Colt. When she
was out of the way of the door, he kicked it hard
so it would slam against the wall. It didn't get
quite that far. He heard a yelp of surprise and
pushed his shoulder against the door to pin the
man behind it who had been hiding there.

He saw someone stand up from where he had
been crouching behind the bed. Morgan's Colt

tracked him and the other man lowered the six-gun he had in his hand.

"You behind the door. I want to hear a gun hit the floor in about two seconds or I start shooting. One . . ."

A gun fell to the floor. Morgan held the door hard against the man.

"You, beside the bed. Lace your fingers together and put your hands on top of your head—now!" The man, who Morgan had never seen before, followed orders. Morgan reached around the door, caught an arm and spun a small man out of the hiding spot.

He had the makings of a black eye and a bruised shoulder that he held gently with his other hand.

Morgan searched both men, then made them lie down on the floor. Then he turned to the woman who hadn't said a word. He patted her down, working all the way up each inner thigh to be sure there was no ankle holster or knife.

She bleated in surprise as he touched her around her private parts but did no more.

"They made me do it," she said. "They told me they would run me out of town if I didn't do this for them."

"What did they pay you?"

"Five dollars." She sighed and collapsed on the bed. Morgan punched the pillow out of the pillowcase and ripped the cloth into long strips three-inches wide. With them he tied the two men on the floor, hands behind their backs, then their ankles. When he finished that he bent the men's feet backward and tied their feet to their wrists. To top it off, he put cloth strips around their mouths so they couldn't yell.

When he finished that, he took the girl's hand and led her out of the room. He closed and locked the door. They key was a skeleton type that should fit any room in the hotel.

He knocked on two doors, found one empty, opened it and pushed the girl inside. He went in, locked the door and tossed the key on the bed.

"They made you do it, you said. Still, it didn't seem like such a bad job, did it? Even if you had to seduce me."

She sighed and sat on the bed. "No, I didn't think it would be such bad work, especially after I saw you. You're a fine hunk of man, good shoulders, narrow hips, a firm handsome face."

She frowned. "Why did you bring me here?"

"Wanted to let you earn your money and finish the job of seducing me."

She smiled for a minute, then the smile faded. "You mean you're not going to take me to the sheriff?"

"What for? No law against asking someone to help you or to invite him into your room."

"Oh, glory!" She reached out and pulled him down so he sat beside her, then she caught his shirt, leaned over and kissed his lips.

"You've been kissed before. How about this way?" She pushed her tongue against his lips until he let her into his mouth. She uttered a small moan as she penetrated him and sagged against him.

His hand closed around one breast, and she caught her breath, then moaned with joy again.

Slowly she pushed him over on the bed and lay on top of him, still holding the kiss. When her lips came off his, she smiled.

"Yes, this is more like it. I don't like guns. I just like to have a man loving me. Is that so bad?"

"Not bad at all," he said. "Some girls even get paid to make love."

"I'm not a whore. Never have been. But I have accepted presents from some of my men friends. Is that so bad?"

His hand still held her breast. She lifted up a little so he could caress it.

She grinned. "I like that. I like you petting my tit that way. I know I'm not supposed to, but I like making love with a man about as much as the man does." She sat up.

"Could you help me get out of this old blouse?"

Morgan sat beside her and undid the buttons.

"It's going to cost you. Who hired you to trap me?"

"Oh, neither one of them. It was a little guy who couldn't have been more than five feet tall. He had a heavy black beard and moustache. Hardly see any of his face. Little beady black eyes. He gave me the five and pointed you out in the dining room. The room clerk was in on it, too."

He finished the buttons and pulled off the blouse. She wore only a thin chemise over her breasts. She flipped it over her head in a second and sat up straight so her breasts thrust forward magnificently.

"Oh, glory but those are fine!" Morgan said. Her breasts were full and large, with cherry pink areolas an inch wide and tiny deep pink nipples centering them. He caught one, rubbed it gently, caressed it and then rolled her nipple between his thumb and finger.

"Oh, glory, yourself!" she said in a small voice.

He could feel the nipple grow and fill with blood as he petted it. Then he bent and kissed the nipple and then around her magic mound.

Kristin gave a yelp of surprise and fell over backwards on the bed, gasping and shivering and shaking. Her whole body spasmed and twisted and vibrated. Then her hips humped upwards against nothing but air. Her back arched, and she let loose with one long low scream of pleasure before she collapsed and pulled him down on top of her.

She tried to say something but couldn't. Her breath came in huge gulping gasps, and her eyes were shut to extend the marvel of her climaxes as long as possible.

Five minutes later, Morgan eased off her soft body and put the room's only straight-backed chair under the door handle. The back two legs were firmly braced on the floor. Anyone trying to come into the room, even with a key, would have to break the chair in half to get inside.

"Come here," she said. He sat on the bed beside her.

"What's your name?"

"Call me Lee."

"Okay, Lee, I want to undress you." She sat up, and her breasts bounced and swayed delightfully. She saw him watching her twin peaks and grinned. "Go ahead, play with them. I like it. Keeps me feeling like fucking."

Morgan laughed. Few women used the word. He sat there and let her take off his shirt. She reveled in the soft reddish brown hair on his chest.

"Men are so beautiful, so perfectly put together. Such strong arms and flat chest and flat belly." She laughed softly. "Then there's the good parts down below."

She stood and unbuckled his belt, then unbuttoned his pants and pulled them down.

"Oh, damn, you have on underdrawers." She'd taken his boots off first and now worked the short underwear down a bit at a time. She kissed it down an inch, worked her fingers along the line and kissed it again, then worked them down more. When she came to his thatch of almost reddish crotch hair up his belly, she squealed and jerked his shorts down quickly.

His erection jolted upward.

Kristen squealed in delight and grabbed it with both hands. Her eyes went wide, and she looked at him.

"Is he all real? So much of him, so. . . ." She giggled and, using one hand, stroked him back and forth.

"Easy," he said.

Kristen giggled again, then stood and stripped out of her skirt and the silk bloomers she wore so she was naked. She posed for him for a moment, turning half around, then back, then she pushed him down on the bed and lay flat on top of him.

"Oh, yes, now this is the way a girl should live. At least get fucked twice a day. Oh, glory!"

She wiggled against him, grinding her crotch against his erection. Then she lifted up so she could see his face clearly.

"Can I be up here the first time? Please? No man has ever let me be on top all the fucking way, and I want to. Please?"

Morgan nodded, and she squealed and lifted her hips and moved around enough to get situated. Then she caught his erection and held it straight up and slowly lowered herself on the shaft, lancing it upward into her.

Kristen squealed as his hot shaft penetrated her, then she began to moan and sigh and move slightly to get positioned just right.

A moment later she lifted on her knees and her hands and began to slide off him and drop down. Each time she fell on his lance she squealed in erotic pleasure. More than a dozen times she did this, and Morgan watched her in amazement. Then she changed her approach and began a lower forward and back movement.

"I'm gonna ride you like a wild stallion on a brand new virgin filly so you get ready for the ride of your life."

She did. The forward and back and up and down motion had Morgan reaching the blasting point before he wanted to. She didn't seem affected by the gyrations, but Morgan could hold back no longer. He bellowed in amazement and punched his hips upward as high as he could, then dropped them, then pounded upward a dozen times as she stopped her own movements and fastened tightly against him.

Before he finished, Kristen brayed in delight and punched hard at him as she soared into a dramatic climax that seemed to keep going on and on. Her body shook and rattled, and she called out in strange words as she worked through the climaxes. At last she sighed and fell on top of him, so spent she could hardly breathe.

She rolled off him at once and lay beside him, holding his hand and panting.

When she could talk again, Kristen leaned up on one arm and looked down at him. "Damn but that was good. Best fucking I've ever done had in my whole life."

"And you've done one or two."

She laughed. "Now don't tease me. You knew I warn't no virgin to start out. Damn but that's some pine tree you got down there between your thighs." She watched him a minute.

"What?

"Oh, nothing. Just woman wishing, I guess. Was wishing I had you all to myself every night. I'd wear you down to a nub in sight of a year, deed I would."

She watched him again. "So what happens now. You not mad at me, are you, for setting you up in the room?"

"No, glad you did. You were so obvious that I knew it was a trap. Somebody else might have fooled me."

"I never was much on the acting part. I do love the lovemaking though. Just so damn good."

They both laughed.

She sat up, and he enjoyed watching her breasts bounce.

"Hey, I don't have to be home no special time, don't have to go home at all, if'n it's all right. Can I stay with you all night?"

"Unless we have some visitors. I don't think they'll find us here. That small man with the beard is going to start wondering where his two killers are pretty soon and come and check on them. Not many hotels in town to look at so he'll be here."

She furrowed her brow in worry. "What happens if he finds you?"

"He'll try to kill me—and I'll kill him."

She shuddered. "Killed as in dead? Those two guys told me they just wanted to talk to you and maybe hit you a few times."

Morgan chuckled. "You think they'd go to all this trouble just to push me around a little. They could do that in a saloon."

They heard loud voices down the hall. Morgan got his pants on and his .45 and cracked the door ajar. He could see down the hall. The two men he had tied up staggered into the passageway. Their feet didn't work right yet. The small man with the beard was there, but he was behind the two hired guns.

"You imbeciles. Can't you do anything right? Two against one and he doesn't even shoot you and still you're beaten. It looks like this is one job I'll have to do myself." The small man with the beard herded his two killers down the steps, and Morgan closed the door gently and locked it.

"At least we're making progress. Now they'll send in the first team of assassins to try to get the job done."

"Why do they want to kill you, Lee?"

"Because they think I know more than I do. So I have to find out what I don't know." He thought of the small package that the dead woman had given him. He had left it in his saddlebags in the livery. Nobody would think to search there for something that evidently was so valuable. He'd have to unseal the package and take a look at it. If it was worth risking his life for, he had the right to find out what it was.

Kristen sat on the bed, then got on her knees, spread them and motioned to him. "Hey, I have an idea how we can try to do it the next time."

Morgan shook his head. "Not a chance. You have to wait until number three. The second time is my choice, and I've got a surprise for you."

It surprised them both.

When Morgan heard someone in the hallway after midnight, he looked out to see two men using a key to get into his room. They went in, lit the lamp and evidently went through his meager belongings. They came out a few minutes later, angry and pushing each other as they went down the hall.

"Boy, Mr. Johnson is gonna be mad as a rooster locked out of the henhouse. You tell him we didn't find nothing. I'm going home and see if my wife still knows me."

Morgan closed the door. When he looked at Kristen she stood on her head on the floor and parted her legs wide.

"Give you any ideas?" she teased from her upside down position.

It did.

They didn't get to sleep that night until nearly five A.M.

Chapter Four

Lee Buckskin Morgan moved all of his belongings from his old room into room 218 just before daylight. The other room had been trashed, his carpetbag upended and everything scattered. His spare Colt .45 was still there, and it looked like nothing had been taken. They didn't find what they wanted.

Morgan put on clean clothes while he watched Kristen sleeping. She had thrown the sheet off her in the warmth of the morning and her long golden hair cascaded around her shoulders, half-hiding one breast but leaving the other one uncovered. Her flat little belly descended into a froth of blonde pubic hair.

Morgan grinned and looked back at the mirror where he had started shaving. He had been trying to work out some kind of a plan for today, but so far he had come up with little. He'd go well out of town and then examine the package that Bernice had asked him to deliver to the China man in Santa Fe. Maybe it was something that could be handled here in town or in Denver which was only a few hours away.

What else? He'd love to meet Brice O'Gallon but had no idea where he lived. He might even be a live-in guard upstairs with the fat man.

"Hey there."

He turned to find Kristen awake and on her hands and knees, letting her heavy breasts swing down like two upside-down mountains. She turned and presented her soft round bottom to him the way many females do in animal mating rituals.

"How about one more to start the day off right?" She giggled and moved her bottom back and forth. "Come on, Lee, don't make me beg. Just come up behind me and pretend you're a big old sheepdog and I'm a bitch in heat." She grinned. "Which I am. Come on."

He wiped the soap off his face with a towel and dropped his pants. He hadn't put on a fresh shirt yet. Morgan went behind her on the bed on his knees and leaned over and grabbed a breast in each hand.

"Damn, you're hard already. How do you get an erection so fast? You must have been playing with me in my sleep."

Morgan grunted and felt her respond as he lanced into her.

"Oh, damn!" she said, then began to climax almost at once as he rode her like a stallion mounting a mare in the pasture. It was quick and fast, and they both exploded at the same time and fell forward panting, not able to talk for a minute. They parted a few minutes later and sat by each other on the bed.

"What do you do here in town?" he asked Kristen.

"Oh, I work at the bank. I'm a bookkeeper, but I don't have to be to work until nine." She grinned. "I'm a friend of the bank manager."

Morgan looked at her. "You ever made love in the bank vault?"

She moved away from him. "What a wild, strange thing to suggest. I'm shocked at you, Lee." Then she broke down laughing and told him just twice, but it was too lumpy.

"We wanted to fuck on a thousand dollars in greenbacks, but they were hard and it wasn't much fun at all."

They parted about seven that morning. Kristen went home to change before she went to work, and Morgan found a small café where he could eat without being on display. He had finished a breakfast of hot cakes and sausage and eggs and coffee when two men came toward him.

He was automatically standing, his hand near his weapon.

The larger of the two waved his hand. "No, no. We're friends. We don't want any trouble. Fact is, we want to help you."

The second man pointed to a door at the back of the small café, and they proceeded into a storage area filled with restaurant supplies.

"Donna Miller tells us that you know something about Fats Johnson that they don't like and that they'll be trying to kill you."

Morgan nodded. "They tried twice yesterday and missed."

"We might be able to help. We're damn tired of being pushed around by the fat man. He owns half the town, but he thinks he owns it all. I've seen three men who opposed him turn up missing—which around here means killed by Fats and his henchmen and buried deep somewhere.

"We figure you can use your gun and give them a run for their money, so we want to help you, if you'll help us."

Lee held out his hand. "Name's Lee Morgan."

The big man took Morgan's hand. "I'm Carl Dunnington. I run the livery stable."

The other man shook hands with Morgan as well. "My name is Travis Gilroy. I'm the sawbones in town. Johnson is going too far. He's working on some big deal and stomping all over the local people. We want him out of here one way or the other."

"I don't do assassinations," Morgan said quickly.

"No, no. We didn't mean that. Johnson owns the sheriff who isn't much good anyway. I'm figuring on getting something we can take to the state attorney general. If we get enough to bring him to trial, it'll be the end of him."

"Are there more than two of you?"

They looked at each other.

"Yes," the doctor said, "but we want it to be a secret. We tried this one time before, and they infiltrated a man into our group. Next thing we knew the top three men in our bunch were either killed or run out of town. We don't want that to happen again."

"Good idea to keep it small with only those men you can trust. But I don't see what I can do."

"We can help you. Whatever you do about Fats

will be good for us. We know the lay of the land here—who can help us and who are afraid to. I understand your room was trashed last night and that you had a shoot-out in the alley yesterday afternoon."

"True."

"Would it help if you knew where Brice O'Gallon lives?"

Morgan grinned and nodded. "I also want to know if there is anyway to get inside the fat man's fortress and how many men he has on guard at night."

"Might take a day or two to find that out," Carl Dunnington said, "but since I'm the livery man in town, I hear a lot of things other folks don't."

"Tell me where O'Gallon lives and I'll see what I can do today to reduce the firepower that the fat man controls. Why don't we meet here for breakfast tomorrow about seven-thirty."

The other two nodded. "Before that I need to take a look at my saddlebags down at the livery stable." Morgan looked up. "Oh, do either of you remember Bernice Upton?"

Both heads came up quickly and nodded. "I found her about ten miles outside of town in a cabin. She'd been shot and died a few minutes after I got there. I understand she figures in this whole picture somehow."

Dr. Gilroy nodded. "Sure does. Prettiest girl in town until she ran off with that no-account. Her pa didn't take it well."

"He worked for the fat man?"

"That's what we heard. They had some powerful bad falling out, and the Uptons took off late one night before Johnson's men got to them."

"Somebody said they went to Denver, but I'd bet they moved farther than that. The fat man owns about half the politicians in Denver, too."

The three men let it stand that way and went out the back entrance to the cafe. Morgan walked with Dunnington through the alley and down a block to the livery stable. His saddlebags were exactly where he had left them, wrapped around the saddle on the peg on the wall.

He took out the package and checked it. It was six inches wide, maybe ten inches long and no more than an inch thick. It had some kind of hard cardboard on the outside and was sealed with wax.

Morgan pushed the package inside his shirt and let the leather vest conceal it. He walked out and waved at the owner, Carl Dunnington, then headed for a patch of heavy brush along the small stream. He was almost out of town here. Only a few small houses nearby. He ducked into the brush and looked out. No one had followed him that he could see.

He used the point of his boot knife, broke the wax seal and pulled back the cardboard. Inside were a batch of papers, all the same size. He sat down and looked them over.

He was no expert, but they looked like some kind of engineering drawings and specifications. What on earth would they be for? Why was Bernice Upton so set on getting them to that Chinaman in Santa Fe?

He stared at the drawings and sets of figures but couldn't understand them. It could be anything, but to Bernice it was something highly important.

All right, he would get the papers to Woo Fan

Too. There was no name or address on the outside of the package, so even that name must be a secret as well. He rewrapped the papers but couldn't put the seal back in place. He'd tie it with string as soon as he got back to the general store.

Morgan didn't know where else to go. Someone knew he was at the hotel; in fact, probably all of Fat Man Johnson's killers knew it by now. It could be a death trap for him, except they didn't know which room he was in.

Morgan went two blocks out of his way and moved up the alley behind the general store. He took his time and made sure that no one saw him. He didn't want to get Mrs. Miller and Lisa into trouble as well.

Morgan thought of the nearly 300 mile trip from Denver down through the mountains to Santa Fe in New Mexico Territory. There used to be one stage that made the run, but he didn't know if it was still working or not. Riding there would take ten days at 30 miles a day. He shook his head. He didn't see any other way.

In the Miller General Store, he saw several customers out front and waited in the rear until they were gone. Then he called softly to Mrs. Miller, who hurried back.

"Heard there was trouble at the hotel last night. Glad to see that you're all right." She looked closer. "What's the matter with your arm?"

He looked down and saw blood on his left upper sleeve. "Oh, I got grazed."

Mrs. Miller grabbed his hand, led him to a chair and sat him down.

"Roll up that sleeve and let's have a look. Doc Gilroy could do it, but he ain't here. I'm near as good as he is."

He had forgotten about the crease that burned a quarter of an inch furrow across the top of his outer arm. He rolled his sleeve up and waited.

She came back with a bottle of whiskey, some salve and some white strips of cloth.

"That whiskey for drinking or sloshing?"

"Pouring delicately, more than likely." She looked at his wound. "Uh huh. You would have been infected in another day. Good thing you bleed." She opened the whiskey bottle and poured whiskey on the wound.

Morgan tensed but didn't utter a sound.

She looked up sharply. "You ain't said nothing. This whiskey or colored water?"

He took the bottle, tipped it and swallowed.

"Whiskey," he said.

"Playing tough guy, I see."

"Where's the princess?"

"Taking her morning nap. That child is too scrawny. My job is to get her fed up proper. She's got pigtails today."

"How far is it to Santa Fe?"

Mrs. Miller looked up quickly. "You're not going to go all the way down there? Must be three hundred miles."

"I made a promise."

"To Bernice?

"Deathbed."

"Don't matter. Don't go."

Morgan looked at her. "You know something I don't?"

"Plenty, young man."

"About Santa Fe and Woo Fan Too."

"That Chinese gentleman will be coming to town to see me in three days."

Morgan took off his hat and wiped his forehead. "Let's get this right. You're telling me that Woo Fan Too is coming here from Santa Fe to see you?"

"That's right."

"Why?"

"He didn't say in his letter this morning, but the only people he knew from this town were the Uptons. I'd make a small wager that the Chinaman coming to town won't please Gunther Johnson one little bit."

"Can he help us any?"

"Depends on what Bernice Upton told you to tell him."

Morgan caught the red ribbon of hard candy Mrs. Miller tossed to him. "She didn't tell me anything to tell him. She gave me a small sealed package and made me promise to take it to him."

Mrs. Miller nodded. "Now we're getting somewhere. What's in the package?"

"How would I know? It's sealed."

"But you looked."

"Yes. Some drawings, some notes, some figures, some kind of specifications or something. Looked like engineer work of some kind, but I'm no expert."

"Me either. There's a man in town who is, but he's probably already on Fat Johnson's payroll. Nobody else we can trust. You have the papers with you?"

"You think I carry something like that around with me? Papers that six or eight people already have been killed trying to protect?"

A customer came in, and Mrs. Miller went toward the front of the store. A moment later two men jumped into the back part of the store both with six-guns out and trained on Morgan.

One of them was five feet tall and had a heavy black beard.

"Well, the elusive Mr. Morgan. So good of you to let us know where you were. I want those papers now. Hand them over and we'll forget I ever saw you."

"What papers, Mr. O'Gallon?"

"No time for games, Morgan. I'll start shooting you in the knees and work up to your crotch until you tell me where they are."

Morgan raised his brows. "Yes, Shorty, from what I've seen of your marksmanship on Bernice Upton, you just might do that—or try at least. You must be a terrible shot."

"Shut up, Morgan. You can't rile me. Where are the papers? I want them, now."

Morgan saw the curtain over the door that led to the front of the store move slightly. That had to be Mrs. Miller. It was time. Now! He dove toward the floor drawing iron as he went down. Two shots thundered in the back room of the Miller General Store. One hit Morgan in the chest, but he wasn't sure where the other shot went. For a moment a black cloud hovered over him, then everything faded away.

Chapter Five

Morgan lay on his left side on the wooden floor. His chest hurt like fire so he knew he couldn't be dead. When the roar of the two shots faded out, he heard O'Gallon talking.

"Mrs. Miller, I've never killed a woman in my life, but I'm tempted. You shot my friend. What am I going to do with you?"

Morgan blinked and saw that O'Gallon stood ten feet away, his six-gun aimed somewhere else, maybe at Mrs. Miller. Morgan looked down at his hand. His right fist still held the Colt. He lifted it, saw the hammer was cocked, centered the sights on O'Gallon's chest and pulled the trigger.

The round jolted through Brice O'Gallon's fancy vest and into his heart where it slammed the small man back against a stack of boxed china.

He died before he slid to the floor.

Morgan sat up, and Mrs. Miller screamed.

She rushed up and knelt beside him. "I thought you were dead. He shot you in the chest and I saw you fall. What in the world?"

Morgan chuckled even though it hurt his chest. He unbuttoned his shirt and reached inside and pulled out the heavy cardboard package. The .45 slug from O'Gallon's gun had torn through the outer cardboard and about half of the sheets of paper.

"Lucky," Morgan said with great restraint.

"No luck, it's a miracle that's come to us right here from God on high. I've never seen nothing like it before." She stood up. "The Lord helps those who help themselves. Our first job is to get these two bodies out of here so they won't be connected with the store. Come on now, no time to dally."

Morgan stood up with only a slight pain in his chest. He had taken quite a thump, but that was a lot better than a .45 slug going halfway through him.

"You shot the other one?" he asked Mrs. Miller.

"You bet. I don't put up with this riffraff. I practice with my .44 every Sunday afternoon."

Morgan found a large wheelbarrow and brought it into the back room. He put the smaller man's body in it, folding him neatly. Then he changed his mind and wrapped him in a cheap blanket from the store, replacing him in the barrow. He threw on top trash and papers and sweepings from the store. Then he wheeled the load out the back door and half a block down where there was a garbage pit.

He dumped the body with the trash and saw that none of the corpse showed.

Morgan did the same thing with the second man, then hauled two more wheelbarrows full of trash to the site to help cover up the bodies.

He was sweating when he finished. Mrs. Miller motioned him into the back room and then into another room where she had her downstairs apartment. She made him wash his hands, then set out a quarter of an apple pie for him and a big mug of hot black coffee.

"When a man does a good job, he gets a good dessert," Mrs. Miller said. She grinned at him, then hurried out toward the front of the store when the bell jangled over the entrance.

She was back soon, sipping her own coffee.

"Both those gunmen will be missed by Johnson," Morgan said.

"Let's hope they didn't tell him they thought you would be coming here. I hope they followed you. Otherwise I'm in a bad batch of trouble."

"I'll stay here tonight and protect you and Lisa. After dark I'll go up the hotel back stairs and get my things from the room. If they're watching it, I'll deal with them."

"Until dark?"

"I'll stay here. Maybe play with Lisa."

Mrs. Miller grinned. "Never seen it to fail. A confirmed, handsome bachelor comes along and loses his heart to a pretty young thing. I think you're a goner, Morgan."

"About the size of it. She's a real beauty, but we can't tell her."

The bell rang again and then a second time, and Mrs. Miller hurried out to check on the customers.

Morgan finished the pie and the coffee, then reloaded his six-gun letting the hammer down on the empty sixth chamber. Lisa came wandering in, rubbing one eye with her small fist.

"Where's Donna?" she asked.

"Busy at the store. You still have your pad and pencils?"

"Yes."

"Can you draw a picture of the man who hurt your mommie?"

"Yes." She sat down and began to draw. It was a stick figure with arms and hands and a dark blob in one hand. The head was a circle, and on it she made a lot of black marks.

"What's all this?" Morgan asked pointing to the marks on the face.

"Silly, that's his beard. He had a black beard."

Morgan thanked her. That was confirmation enough that O'Gallon had indeed killed her mother. He asked if she could draw a picture of a horse and a house, and it went on that way until Mrs. Miller was free to come back in.

"I think I'll close up early today. You probably want a big supper. Fact is I might be able to eat a good meal myself. Of course I need to cook healthy food for Lisa."

"I can help cook. I helped my mommie cook."

Mrs. Miller beamed and assured Lisa she could help. Morgan got the idea little Lisa could do just about anything she wanted to in this new home he had found for her.

So the child was taken care of. Mr. Woo would be coming to town so he could deliver the engineering drawings to him. Today he had killed the man who had shot down Bernice Upton. His work here was nearly done. That's when he thought about the two men he had met that morning. He'd work with them at least until Woo Fan Too arrived. He wondered if he should tell them about the papers, but he decided not to. He might not even turn them over to the Chinaman until he had some idea what they were.

Morgan nodded, stretched out on a sofa and caught a small nap.

In the second floor office, apartment and fortress of Gunther Johnson over the hardware store, a serious meeting took place.

"What the hell you mean you haven't seen Shorty O'Gallon," the fat man roared. He lay in a big chair that had been custom-made for him. The back let down so he could sleep there if he wanted to. It had six swivel wheels on it, three sets of special ball-bearing wheels that rolled smoothly anywhere in the second floor layout.

A slender man stood in front of the desk, his hat turning around and around in his nervous hands. "Slim, you work for O'Gallon. Where is he?"

"Said he had an idea where he might be able to find that Morgan guy who put up them posters. He took Crunch with him, and they left."

Johnson's face turned red; his small eyes almost closed as he glared at the tall man near the door. "Slim, you get the hell out of here and don't come back until you find O'Gallon. Tell him he's in a whole lot of trouble. Now get out!"

Gunther Johnson wiped his forehead with a linen handkerchief.

"Incompetents! Nothing but a bunch of boobs around here. Why can't I find smart men to work with me? Damn, never get anything done unless I do it myself. Push me up to the desk," he commanded.

A midget, who was perfectly proportioned and stood only 30 inches tall, jumped off a stool and pushed the big chair forward to a massive desk built high enough so Johnson's legs and the arms of the chair slid under the top. He grunted at the midget who returned to his stool and a book he had been reading.

Johnson looked around his desk. It was neat, but busy. He had two small wooden trays big enough to hold letter-sized paper. Both were marked "IN" and both had piles of paper in them.

Gunther Johnson snorted at something he read, then pushed on the edge of the desk and swiveled the chair around.

"Midge, get on your horse and go get Halstead. No excuses. If he has a client, kick him out. Tell him unless he's got his pants down in the outhouse, I want him in here in two minutes."

Midge nodded, put a bookmark in his place and ran to the door. He had to stretch to get his hand to the doorknob, but he opened it and vanished to the other side.

Johnson grunted his approval. Midge was the best man he had, including Halstead. The damn lawyer had been getting sloppy lately, and he had slowed down. Five years ago he was a ball of fire. Now he was half burned out. That damn young wife had done it to him. A man in his late forties shouldn't fuck so much. He said she'd been at him at least once a day for almost a year now. Burn out a man's balls.

Johnson swung back to the desk and scribbled notes on two sheets of paper before the door opened behind him.

"Halstead coming on board," the lawyer said as he came toward the big man's back.

Johnson swung around.

"Did you get them signed?" Johnson demanded.

"Most of them. Three of them are holding out. They know someone is after the whole area, and they're getting curious. I figure if one of them gets burned out, the other two will come around."

"Get it done as soon as you can. The more we can do now, the more money we make. You heard anything more about this Morgan guy?"

"Little. Evidently he stumbled onto the cabin where the Upton woman was. O'Gallon said she was almost dead when he left her. She must have told Morgan something, and he grabbed the small girl and came to town. He went from knowing nothing to knowing too damn much. Your hotshot gunmen haven't fared well against him."

"What about the package?" Johnson demanded. "Does he have it or doesn't he?"

"O'Gallon said he had the man pinned down and would finish it off today. Is he back yet?"

"No. He's overdue."

"Not another failure. We've got to hire better guys with a gun. Where did O'Gallon go after this Morgan?"

"We don't know. He didn't say. Forget him for now. We still have a lot of work to do. The Governor will be in town on Friday. This is Tuesday. We've got to have the last of those parcels tied up by then."

"We will," the lawyer said. "But what good will they be without the package?"

"Land is always good to own. If it doesn't happen with us this time, then it will the next time. We'll still be in the commanding position by owning that land."

Halstead nodded. He was not a large man, and at 48 he seemed to have slowed down. He had sharp features and thinning brown hair and a high forehead. He wore a dark suit and vest with a gold chain and gold watch. His pants were creased.

"If we don't get the package, we go into a time holding pattern, but what happens if somebody else gets the package and knows what it is and uses it?"

Johnson stared at the smaller man. "That would be a large problem. Not even the Governor has considered that happening. That would cut us out of ninety-five percent of the potential profits."

Halstead checked his fingernails which were polished and trimmed. "So our first job is to get this Morgan guy, and if he doesn't have the package we cut him apart an inch at a time until he tells us where he stashed it. There isn't any alternative. We must have that package!"

Johnson waved at Midge. "Bring in those two men in the holding room. Halstead, you go out and round us up six more guns. I don't care how good they are, just so they can stand and shoot. Give 'em two dollars a day."

Halstead bobbed his head and left. The midget returned a moment later with two men in tow. Both wore range clothes, and both had six-guns in holsters that hung low on their thighs.

"Morgan is the man we want. You two check the hotel and find out if he's registered. Then see if his gear is still in the room. This gent is about six feet tall, clean shaven, reddish brown hair.

Go find him. I want him dead or alive. Whoever brings him in earns himself a hundred dollar bonus."

The two men grinned and hurried out the door, checking their hardware to be sure the weapons were in place.

What next? Johnson cuffed papers around on his desk, then looked long and with interest at a map on the wall. It was the rugged territory around Denver and showed the Rocky Mountains all the way to Cheyenne.

He checked his watch and nodded. "Midge, it's noon; let's have something to eat."

Midge came and rolled the chair away from the desk, then through a door and into a hall. They went to the back of the second floor where a table was set for two. The table was high enough so the chair and the arms slid in neatly under it.

Midge climbed onto a tall stool and rang a small dinner bell.

Two cooks in white jackets and hats hurried into the room. Each carried a large covered tray. They placed the trays on the table, and a small man with steel blue eyes, a black pencil-thin moustache and darting hands opened the silver serving dishes.

"Ah, gentlemen. Today we have roast duck in a fine wine sauce and a half dozen vegetables cooked in butter with a cheese sauce. Mashed potatoes and an excellent wine and mustard gravy—and for a special treat, fresh frog's legs, fried in butter and garlic. The desert will be along later."

He was a small Frenchman Johnson had hired though an ad in a Paris newspaper at a ridiculously high salary and brought him to Colorado a year ago. He was a superb chef, and Johnson was gaining more weight by the week.

The midget avoided the roast duck, concentrating on the frog legs.

Johnson snorted. "Midge, how in hell do you eat so much and never gain a pound? I swear you're getting skinnier by the day."

The small man looked up and wiped his fingers on his linen napkin. "Mr. Johnson, I am what the cattlemen would call a hard feeder. Put me on a meadow of lush grass and I could eat away all summer and never get fat enough for market. It's just my nature. That's also what makes me so efficient, loyal and such a good companion."

"You left out modest," Johnson said as he tore a wing off the duck and proceeded to reduce it to a few bones. He ate with his hands and with a large spoon. How he ate wasn't important, getting enough food in his belly to support his 384 pounds was the vital part of eating.

He had four meals a day, plus three snacks. He kept the cook and his two assistants on duty 18 hours a day. The cooks had standing orders for fish and shellfish from Boston once a week. They were shipped in a wooden box filled with solid chunks of ice.

Two local men were employed full time and provided game and birds on demand. Sometimes when venison was ordered a deer would be brought in and the big man would eat only one meal from it.

Early on the cooks had learned to sell off all but a quarter of any large game animal brought in. Johnson never thought to ask what happened to the rest of the meat.

The midget tasted the red wine and sipped it
as he ate. He was not a big eater, but for his
size he did eat a lot. He was finished long before
Johnson. The midget sat there waiting. It did not
occur to him to leave the table before his employ-
er was finished.

"Midge, how long have you been with me?"

"Almost nine years, Mr. Johnson. You hired
me in Denver and we came here in July, I think
it was."

"No regrets?"

"Other than not finding a wife, none. You treat
me well. I have all the comforts I want."

"But no wife, no sex. I have loaned you one of
my girls from time to time."

"I thank you for that, but it's not the same."

"We could advertise for a bride in Denver or
San Francisco."

"Sir, may I express my feelings?"

"Of course."

"When I find a bride, it will be by my own hand.
I appreciate your offer. To marry is important to
me, but I must find my own bride. It's a super-
stition with me."

"Subject closed. What do you think happened
to Mr. O'Gallon?"

"From reports by others who have met this
Morgan, I'd say that O'Gallon made one mistake
and he's now dead."

Johnson looked up sharply. "Dead?"

"Yes. This Morgan has proved to be a gunsharp.
He's extremely good with his weapons from what
men who have survived meeting him have told
us."

"I figured he was just a drifter. We must find
him before dark and get the package so all will

be ready when the Governor arrives Friday."

Dinner was over and Midge rolled the fat man back to his front window where he looked out through thin curtains at the street below. He hadn't been down the ramp at the back for a year.

"My little town will be much larger soon, Midge. I'm going to make it an important part of Colorado. But first we need that damn package!"

They moved back to the office and the desk. A moment later Halstead came into the room. His tie was askew, he was breathing hard, and sweat beaded his forehead.

"I only could get four men," he said as he fanned himself with a magazine. "The men said it was too dangerous working for you for two dollars a day. I offered three dollars and then four dollars and at last got four men.

"I asked why they thought it was too dangerous. They told me that somebody had just found two of your guards. Brice O'Gallon and his partner had both been shot dead, thrown in a dump behind Main Street and half covered with garbage."

"Morgan?"

"Sounds like it. We know he's good with a gun."

"Damn! Send those four men out on the street watching for Morgan. Use the best description we've got. Talk to any of our men who have seen him. We've got to kill him and get that package from him. We've got to kill him and get that package from him before sundown."

Chapter Six

Later that same afternoon, Morgan got tired of sitting around the back of the store. He found a slouch hat that came down over part of his face and made him look quite different. He took off his leather vest, shifted his six-gun so it rode high on his thigh and undid the tie-down thong. That should make him look different enough.

Mrs. Miller watched him a minute, went to a counter and brought back something. "Try these on," she said. "The lenses are just plain glass. Part of some costume things I have."

She held out a pair of glasses with heavy black rims. He put them on and looked in a mirror. The glasses made him look so different that he barely recognized himself.

Morgan chuckled. "That should make me into a new man. Getting all tied up sitting around here.

When did you say that Chinaman would be in town?"

"Tomorrow evening if all goes well. With that stage coach line you never can tell. They get washouts and rock slides; even some Indians down there ain't too friendly."

At the back door, Donna Miller touched his arm. "You be careful out there. Gunther Johnson wants you dead, so watch your step."

"I aim to do that. You take care of that little girl." Morgan opened the back door and walked north away from the garbage pit where he had dumped the two bodies. He'd heard some activity down there earlier and saw some men lift out the two bodies. So now Johnson would know.

He cut back to town, looked in the window of the bank but didn't see Kristen. He went inside and saw her in back of a desk with two huge account books in front of her. He left without catching her attention.

He drifted on down the street wondering if Johnson had men out gunning for him. Probably. What was so important about those engineering drawings? He couldn't fathom it. If he could read the drawings and the notes he could work up an idea. The package was still under his shirt. He figured it had saved his life once so he should just leave it there. This way he didn't have to worry about hiding it and having somebody steal it.

He walked deliberately in front of the hardware store, knowing that just overhead somewhere Gunther Johnson was wringing his hands and plotting how to get rid of this sudden thorn in his side. Even after Woo Fan Too came, Morgan decided he might stick around and see how this little caper came out.

First he'd check out this Mr. Woo and see if he was honest. There could be some kind of inheritance for little Lisa from those engineering papers. It might have to be handled delicately. Mr. Woo from Santa Fe might not be the right man to look out for the girl's future.

He had no idea how much the engineering drawings might be worth. If they were for a tall stone building somewhere, they could be worth thousands of dollars. He wished he could find out, but asking advice would give himself away. He'd just have to wait and watch and do what he could.

He turned into a small café and slipped into a back booth. That was before he saw that a young lady also sat there on the other side.

"Oh, excuse me, I didn't see you," Morgan said.

She was young and pretty, and the coffee cup was almost lifted to soft lips. She lowered the cup and watched him a moment, then extended her small right hand. The nails had been buffed and carefully tended. He shook her hand.

"I'm Piper Halstead," she said, her voice firm and confident.

"Hello, Piper Halstead. My name is Judson Jones. Pleased to meet you." He had no idea why he gave her a fake name. It was triggered automatically when she said her name was Halstead. Her father apparently was the lawyer working for Johnson. No sense spraying his name around this town. Halstead and Johnson both probably knew it already.

She watched him a moment, then grinned. "I'm quick when it comes to evaluating people. That's why it took me almost three seconds to see that you're a gentleman and that you're here for a quick cup of coffee, and you wanted the back booth so not everyone in town would know you were here."

Morgan let go of her hand reluctantly. She smiled, and it set off bells in the back of his mind. She wasn't just pretty; she was beautiful, with soft brown hair, long lashes, a pert, cute little face and cheekbones set high. The combination was something to behold.

"Pardon me for staring at you, but I'm a slow study. It took me, oh, twenty, thirty seconds to appreciate just how beautiful you are. I'm stunned and trying to catch my breath."

She smiled. "I'll share the booth with you, Mr. Jones. You don't need to go to all that flattery. Really. I was almost hoping that somebody would come. What do you do in town?"

"Oh, I'm on my way through, really. I'm a businessman from Denver looking for a good place to start my next store, but I don't think this is the town."

"Why not? We're growing. We have a few ranchers around, and a little lumber sawmill is starting, and before long we'll be on a traveled route from the east."

She laughed and covered her face with her hands. "I'm starting to sound like my father talking to a client to start a business here. But really, it's a fine little town."

"What do you do, Piper, beside promote the town?"

"Oh, I don't have any work. Mostly I go to club meetings and work with the Missionary Society at church, then I help at dinners for Daddy. My mother passed on a few years ago."

"So you're hostess for your father. That must be quite a job. Today you just felt like running out of the house and having a walk downtown."

"Right! How did you know? Sometimes it gets lonesome up in that house. It's nice, but I don't have a lot of friends in town. Not a lot of girls my age."

"Nineteen," he guessed.

"Oh, no, I'm just past twenty." She paused. "That seems old to me, but to you that's not old at all."

"True. I'm a few years older than twenty."

A waitress came, and he ordered coffee. "Do you like cherry pie?" he asked Piper. She nodded.

"But I shouldn't."

"Of course not. Neither should I, but that's what makes a little fling like this worthwhile. It will spoil our dinner and make us feel guilty, but it will taste just delicious. I saw the pie when I came in."

Morgan looked at the waitress. "Bring us two pieces of that cherry pie."

"Oh, but . . ." Piper looked at the waitress, then back at Morgan and shrugged.

"I guess it will be all right."

When the waitress left, Morgan looked over at her. "I bet you do a lot of reading."

"Yes, we get the Denver newspaper, the *Rocky Mountain News*, and then some magazines. Oh, and we're starting a library here in town. I'm going to help set it up. My father is donating fifty books. It will make a hole in his own library, but he decided someone else might want to read them—and I just bet they will."

When the waitress served the pie, he had a bite of it and then she did and then they both nodded. It was good pie.

"What kind of a store are you going to open?"

"That's the beauty of it. I don't know. I figured I'd find a small town that needed some kind of store. Say there wasn't a livery stable, or it needed a bank or maybe a hardware store. I could start whichever kind was needed. But from the looks of this town here, there isn't any one kind of store that you need."

"Oh, my father always says that Lafayette needs a good haberdashery, a men's store. But he says there aren't enough men in town who would buy clothes there to make it pay."

"Still, that's a good idea. I'll consider that one."

"Good, I'll tell Daddy. He'll be pleased."

The girl came back and refilled their coffee cups.

"Well, looks like we have had coffee and pie together," Piper said. "I do hope the gossips don't hear of this."

"I doubt if this will interest them when they have so much else to talk about," Morgan said with a touch of sarcasm.

Piper grinned. "You are outspoken, aren't you? Where are your from? Denver, did you say?"

"Denver and more. Idaho some. You lived here all your life?"

"Oh, no. We came from Chicago and stopped in Omaha, then on to Denver. We've been here in Lafayette for six years now."

She finished another sip of coffee and slid out of the booth. "I really should be going."

He stood as well. "Miss Piper Halstead, it was good to meet you. Could I come calling at your home one of these days?"

She blushed and shook her head and turned to see if anyone were listening. "Oh, no. I mean

Daddy works in his office and all. Maybe I'll see you again here for coffee sometime."

"How about tomorrow at three," Morgan said.

"Well, why not? Yes. I'd enjoy that. You can tell me about Idaho. I've never been there." She held out her delicate hand. "Good-bye, Mr. Jones. And thank you for the pie." As she turned and walked away, Morgan was delighted by the gentle way that her hips swayed under the print dress.

He paid his tab and left the café. He could not see Piper when he looked in both directions.

He checked his pocket watch and saw it was five minutes after three. Morgan moved down the boardwalk easily, with an efficient stride that wasn't hurried. He passed the bank, and when he looked in the window, he saw that the chair where Kristen had been sitting was empty.

A moment later someone hurried from the side of the bank and put an insistent arm through his. He saw Kristen beside him with a hat that half-covered her face.

"Just keep on walking and I won't tell anyone who you are. Are you crazy walking down the street? There are eight or ten armed men roaming through town searching everywhere for you. They tore up the room you used to have in the hotel. Lord only knows how many more there are by now. In case you hadn't heard, there's a hundred dollar cash reward for you, dead or alive."

She hurried him down the first side street, and he felt her relax a little.

"You think that hat and glasses are going to fool many people?"

"Has so far. You know me a little more intimately than most of the people in town."

She flashed him a grin. "That I do, and I don't

want you to go to waste in some grave." She
kept them walking toward the residential part of
town.

"Where are we going?"

"Time you got off the street. Not many people
know where I live. I decided you need to be hidden. I saw you earlier when you came in the bank.
Did you see Burel Halstead waiting in line at the
teller's window? The man would have pissed in
his pants if he knew you were right there near
him."

Morgan laughed. "You talk this wild all the
time?"

"Only when I'm worried and a little mad and
getting just terribly sexy hot and wanting you
and afraid that they would shoot you first before
I got you safely in my bed and between my naked
thighs again."

"Now that is more like the Kristen we know and
love."

"And fuck."

"Yes, and fuck. How much farther?"

"Another block. I think I can hold out, but if
I can't, you just plunge right in if I drop on my
back in the next yard and spread my legs."

"You probably won't do that. Your banker friend
would have to fire you, and then he couldn't get
you after work anymore. Might be best to hold
your legs together until we get inside."

"Where have you been for the past half hour?
I've been there by the bank waiting for you."

"Oh, I had a piece of cherry pie and coffee."

"Where?"

"Some little café. I was with Piper Halstead."

Kristen spun him around, her eyes wide. "You
didn't give her your right name?"

"Fact is, I didn't. Would she have told her daddy?"

"Of course. The girl is a virgin and more than anxious to get married."

"I'm not a candidate."

"Somehow I figured that. Here's my door."

It was a small frame house with no picket fence but with a natural yard that had been mown recently. There were two rose bushes trying to bloom and a pair of spindly hollyhocks shooting up nearly six feet near the door. Lilacs bloomed on the other side of the door. She caught a spray, snapped it off and took it inside. The door had not been locked.

"You always leave your door unlocked?"

"Usually. Nothing inside to steal. Nobody in town steals anything anyway. This is not a big city."

She turned, caught his face in both hands and kissed him. As she did she pushed her lush body hard against his from hips to surging breasts. She sighed as she let him go.

"Oh, yes, now there is a promise. But tonight, you're going to have to earn it. You have to wine and dine me, here at home. You have to serve me supper, and then a glass of wine, and you have to bring me flowers. Then after you get me in the proper mood, you have to seduce me, slowly and gently like I'm the first virgin you ever destroyed. You want to do that?"

He nodded.

"Otherwise forget everything I said and we can strip right here on the floor and I'll fuck your brains out."

Morgan laughed. "You are a little bit crazy, and I love it. Let's try dinner and wine and flowers and see what happens. But not too slowly. As soon as it gets dark, I have work to do."

They cooked a light supper and opened a bottle of wine. Morgan picked more lilacs, put them in a vase and presented them to her.

In her bedroom later, the lovemaking was so soft and tender that Kristen cried. She didn't want to let him go when the deep shadows stole across the room.

"Just once more," she begged.

He kissed her lightly on each bare breast, then on her lips and dressed.

"You'll come back tonight?"

"I might. Lock your front door but leave the back one open. If I come, it won't be until late."

He reshaped the hat so it rode higher on his head, dropped his gunbelt down a notch to where it belonged and tied the bottom of the holster tightly to his thigh with the leather thong. The tie-down could make a big difference in a quick draw.

When his hand hit the butt of the weapon to lift it out of its leather home, the holster could move upward a half-inch from the force of the pull on the iron. By tying down the leather, it would not move at all. This meant on a fast draw the muzzle of the Colt would clear the top of the holster a half-inch quicker. He could point it at the target, thumb back the trigger and shoot that much faster.

Sometimes in a gunfight that half-inch of space could be the difference between shooting first and turning up dead.

He walked back to town and studied the fire escape of the Princess Hotel. It was fully dark now, and it took Morgan less than five minutes to spot the guard on the fire escape. He had positioned himself directly under the wooden steps that went up the back of the structure to the second floor and then the third floor windows.

The only way to get to him was to come around the far side of the building and walk up on the man where he hid. Either that or throw a knife, and Morgan didn't have that much knife throwing experience. Now if he had his black snake whip he could do the job silently but he had lost his a month ago.

Morgan did the only thing he could; he faked it. He went to the side of the hotel and walked down the vacant lot to the corner then stepped around in plain sight of the guard.

"Hey, you there?"

"Yeah—and shut up," a voice came back.

"Got to talk. New orders." Morgan walked along the back of the building, his right hand behind his hip with the Colt ready for anything.

He got within three feet of the man before the darkness revealed a cowboy sitting on a box with a cupped cigarette in his right fist.

"What the hell? I don't know . . ." When Morgan powered the heavy Colt down on the top of the guard's head, his eyes glazed and he tipped over on his back, unconscious.

Morgan tied him up, gagged him, then quietly went up the wooden stairs. He stopped at the first window and looked inside. It was the second floor. He saw no guards in the dimly lighted corridor.

He pushed up on the window and found that it moved silently. A moment later, he had stepped inside, the Colt still in his right hand. He remembered the room, if only the management had not rented it again.

He knocked on it lightly. No response. He tried the handle. Locked. Morgan used the key, opened the door and slid inside. He lit a match, and in the sudden glare he saw a maniacal face and the muzzle of a shotgun.

Morgan flipped the match away, fired with his six-gun and dove to one side in the space of a heartbeat, just before a shotgun blasted. The twin explosions of the two weapons in the small room were like walking inside a bass drum being pounded. Morgan's ears felt as if they had been run over by a thousand head of stampeding steers.

At least the shotgun pellets had missed him. He didn't dare cock his gun for a second shot. The man might still be alive and waiting. He reached in his pocket, found a quarter and threw it at the slice of light that he figured must be the window. It hit the window and bounced to the floor. No reaction. Morgan moved silently toward where he had seen the man sitting on the bed. Morgan hit a pair of boots and felt upward to find knees. The man didn't move.

Morgan scraped another match on the wooden floor. He saw the gunman sprawled on his back on the bed with half his face shot away by the big .45 slug from the Colt.

Morgan found his carpetbag. He lit one more match to be sure he had everything, then dropped the bag out the window into the open space at the far side of the hotel. He holstered his weapon, then crawled through the second story window.

It took him five minutes to crawl down six feet on the side of the building using every handhold he could find. Then there were no more. He hung by his hands and dropped into the darkness.

His feet had been less than four feet from the ground. Morgan found his suitcase and sprinted away from the hotel past the rear where he figured the guard would still be tied up.

Morgan ran for a block and slowed down. No one had followed him. He paused, wondering where he was heading. He shrugged. He told Mrs. Miller he would be back there for the night, and he'd better stick to that plan. He'd get a good nights sleep that way and be ready for whatever came tomorrow.

Morgan went in the back door of the general store that had been left unlocked. He fastened the inside lock and turned toward the backroom when he heard a piercing scream. He dropped his carpetbag, pulled the comforting Colt .45 into his hand and ran as silently as he could toward the apartment in back from where the scream had come.

Chapter Seven

Morgan ran toward the general store's back apartment and slowed down when he heard a low voice.

"Mrs. Miller, we know he was here. We got witnesses who saw this Morgan come in and go out the back door. Don't lie to me or your store just might burn right to the ground. You tell me where he went and when he's coming back, and you won't get hurt none."

Morgan eased up to the wall and peered around the doorway into the first floor apartment. All he could see was the living room. He pushed farther around and looked the whole room over then dodged back.

Nobody in the living room. They had to be in the kitchen. It was a big kitchen with a table and one of the new wood-burning ranges that had a removable top and a hot water heating coil.

He stepped into the living room and looked into the small slice of the kitchen he could see. He saw only the range and some cupboards. The people must be near the table. He moved slowly across the room to the far wall and then edged up to the kitchen door.

When he looked inside, he saw one man bending over Mrs. Miller. She had been tied to a chair. The man with his back to Morgan held a gun in one hand and with the other he stroked Mrs. Miller's breasts.

"Don't do that; it won't help you," she said. "If I knew where he went I'd tell you."

"You're getting hot, Mrs. Miller. You been without a man a long time. I bet you'd suck it off for me right now, but I ain't got the time. Tell me now where he is, or I start twisting this tit until you scream your mouth off."

"I told you. I don't know."

That was when four-year-old Lisa suddenly ran in from the other room off the kitchen that had become her bedroom. Her long blonde hair flew as she rushed to her new mother.

"Mommie, Mommie, I'm hungry."

The big man with the gun took a step back. "Who the hell is this?"

"Friend of mine. I'm keeping while her ma is away."

"Yeah, I bet." He bent to grab the child.

Morgan bolted from the doorway, his boots crashing into the floor to make as much noise as he could. The gunman spun as Morgan knew he would with the gun up. Morgan's Colt had been aimed since he began his charge. He fired well before the other man's weapon was far enough around to gain a target.

The roar of the Colt in the room was like a thunderclap a dozen times over. Lisa wailed and held her hands over both her ears. Mrs. Miller winced and waited for the noise to fade.

Morgan watched the slug from his .45 slide under the gunman's upraised arm, catch him in the side and drive straight through his lungs and into his heart, dumping him onto the floor.

Morgan rushed in, picked up Lisa and held her, then with his other hand he untied Mrs. Miller.

Without a word the woman took the child. Morgan checked the body on the floor. The gunman was dead. Morgan grabbed the boots of the dead man and dragged him through the back rooms to the alley. There on the small dock, Morgan swung the body over his shoulder and carried it down to the dump. He pitched the man into the hole and walked back, scuffing out his boot prints on the way.

On the dock, he checked and found only a spot or two of blood. He rubbed them with dirt until they couldn't be seen, then went inside.

Mrs. Miller held the child and rocked her gently. There was no alarm or shock in the woman's eyes. She was telling a story of some kind to the little girl. They went to the stove and found a cookie from the jar, then Mrs. Miller carried the small bundle back into the bedroom.

Morgan found lye soap, a brush and an old towel and cleaned the blood off the wooden kitchen floor. There wasn't much. The bullet had been spent enough so it never came out of the body.

Once he had the blood cleaned up, Morgan put away the brush and towel. Mrs. Miller came out of the room and closed the door.

"Thanks," she said.

"Thank you. I swear I don't know how he knew I had been here."

"Don't matter. You can't stay here now."

"I've got my things from the hotel. I'll find a place. Might stay along the river. Got a spare blanket?"

She took one off the couch and rolled it for him.

"You still have the papers?"

He nodded.

"Good. Now all you have to do is stay alive until Woo Fan Too gets here tomorrow. Think you can do that?"

"I can. I was thinking we might not want to turn over the papers right away. They could be worth something. If they are, the cash should go to little Lisa. If her granddad did something good, she should get the rewards. Sound like a reasonable idea?"

Mrs. Miller nodded. "I was kind of thinking the same thing. Anything worth this many lives must be worth one hell of a lot of money to somebody. When the Chinaman comes to see me, I'll try to find out what he's come for and exactly what all of this is about. Might work."

"I better get out of here. Have I left anything that could tie me in here?"

She shook her head. "The man with the big hands tried to find something of yours. He didn't. You take care. I'll see you tomorrow afternoon at the front door. These are back door killers. They don't like to work out in the open."

Morgan waved at her, took his carpetbag and hurried out the back door. He waited for her to lock it, then worked his way up the alley in the shadows like a black bird on a cloudy night.

Ten minutes later, he eased in the back door of Kristen's house. There was a light on in the kitchen. He carried the lamp into the bedroom where another light burned. She sat up when she heard him come.

As usual, Kristen wore nothing at all in bed.

"Lee?"

"Yes." He put down the second lamp.

"Is everything all right?"

He told her what happened back at the general store.

"You poor darling. What you need is a good night's sleep. I promise not to seduce you. I might snuggle against your back, but I don't want you worn out for tomorrow. You can stay here all day. Just lay low and wait them out. They'll get tired of looking for you soon." She frowned.

"Why are they so insistent on finding you? Does it have anything to do with that package you carry inside your shirt?"

"If you don't know anything, they can't make you tell them anything. I wouldn't put it past them to figure out that since they used you once, they might want to try to use you again. Have you seen Rocky Paulson lately? He's probably the best gun that Johnson has left. If you see him, get out of sight somewhere in the bank."

"The bank? I can't go to work tomorrow."

"Of course you can. If you don't, the banker will know something is wrong and might come here hunting you. Then the whole town would know. You go to the bank just as usual, and don't come home until you usually do."

"Sometimes I walk home for dinner at noon."

"Don't tomorrow. I have a hunch they'll be watching you."

He sat on the edge of the bed and stripped off his boots, then his clothes. He crawled into bed beside her naked, lovely body wearing only his underwear. She grinned and put one arm over him.

"I'm ready to go to sleep if you are." She said it once more, then smiled when she heard the strong even breathing that she knew meant he was already asleep.

Morgan awakened at six A.M., dressed and had breakfast ready when Kristen came out of the bedroom about seven. She was sleepy-eyed and naked, and Morgan grinned at her marvelous figure. Surging breasts almost ready to sag a little from their own weight, a slender, pinched-in waist, sleek hips with a blonde forest at her crotch and then deliciously carved legs, slender and strong. She had the most perfect figure he'd ever seen. Everything was in the right proportion, and over it all was a delightfully beautiful face.

She grinned.

"You're staring."

"I was thinking what a wonderful way to start the morning, just being able to stare at you all naked and sexy. I've got breakfast ready for you."

"Shall I eat naked?"

"Your house, do what you want. Of course, I'd be pleasured no end if you did. Why cover up a beautiful body like yours?"

A half hour later she kissed him lightly on the cheek and walked with a gentle little swish of her naked bottom as she went into the bedroom to get dressed.

Morgan put the dirty dishes on the counter next to the stove. He'd do them later if he had time.

Time was what he had a lot of today. He wasn't sure if he should venture out of the house.

Then he remembered his date for coffee with pretty little Piper Halstead that afternoon at three. He grinned. She was as cute as a newborn filly. Yes, he'd try to see her, unless the town was an armed camp bristling with bounty hunters.

When Kristen came back a few minutes later, she wore a dress that swept the floor and covered her from neck to wrists.

Morgan scowled. "Damn waste, covering up a beautiful figure like that. I can't even see your breasts."

Kristen glowed with the compliment. "That's the way it's supposed to be. It's our backward society. It will be five hundred years before we have naked bankers, and then only on the warm summer days." She laughed thinking about it.

He kissed her lips lightly. "Now you get to work and act as if nothing has happened. I don't know what else they might try. If Halstead or some of Johnson's men try to question you, you scream and call for the bank guard."

"We don't have a bank guard."

"Then just scream. The men in the bank will charge to your rescue."

She laughed softly. "You are a nice man. Could I keep you a while as a pet?"

"Possible. Would you feed me well and take care of all of my needs?"

"I'd try, but sometimes you get so sexy I don't know if one woman could satisfy you."

"We can always test out your theory for a few days."

She smiled, kissed him on the cheek and hurried out the door.

Morgan washed the dirty dishes automatically and put everything away. Then he stared out the windows but could see little from there. He stormed around the house for a half hour, but he knew he couldn't go check on Lisa and Mrs. Miller.

Hard telling what Johnson's men would do during daylight. It would slow them down a little. Like Mrs. Miller said, they were back door killers, night workers. Daylight made them more cautious.

He dropped onto a couch in the living room, stretched out, put a pillow under his head and folded his arms across his chest. Best way to kill time was to work it to death. His father had told him that. No more work to do, so he'd take the next best course and have a nap.

He closed his eyes, and for a moment all he could see was the luscious, naked body of Kristen. She was a gem. Most women were out of proportion somewhere—hips too large or breasts not large enough or legs too long. Kristen was the most perfect figure he'd ever seen. Her big tits didn't hurt anything either.

Morgan grinned and closed his eyes. He came awake when someone knocked on the front door. He rose without a sound, drew his Colt and moved so he could see out the front window. There wasn't quite the right angle so he could not see who stood at the door.

The knocking came again, six sharp raps as if from the butt of a six-gun. Then the man grumbled and turned away. Morgan recognized Rocky Paulson who walked out to the street, looked back at the house, then turned and headed for the downtown area.

If Paulson wanted to see Kristen, why didn't he go to the bank? Maybe he did, and Kristen wasn't there. Why wouldn't she be there? Morgan paced the living room. He checked a clock on the living room table. It was eleven-thirty. He'd had a three hour nap.

Morgan found some cheese, made a two egg cheese omelet and squeezed it between two slices of homemade bread. Best sandwich he'd had in weeks. He had made the smallest of fires in the wood-burning range so there would be almost no smoke coming from the chimney. He didn't make coffee for the same reason. If Paulson looked at the house and saw smoke coming from the chimney after finding nobody to answer the door, he'd be back with some partners.

A half hour later, Morgan knew he had to get out of the house. It felt like a prison. He found some strips of white cloth and used them to bandage half of his face, covering one eye and wrapping the strips around his chin and over his head. When he had one eye covered and half his face blanked out, he tied off the bandage. In the cupboard he found a small bottle of catsup and painted a soft red stain on the jaw side of his bandage.

Then he put his dark rimmed glasses on and checked in the mirror. No chance anyone could recognize him. He found the slouch hat, crumpled it up even more, then put it on. He took off his vest and put on a clean shirt, a light blue one to go with his working style jeans. He cinched his gun belt up a notch and untied the laces at the bottom of the holster. Now, he'd be nearly invisible to someone hunting Lee Morgan.

He walked Main Street on both sides. Nobody paid him any attention. He stopped in at the doctor's office and saw that it was an old fashioned arrangement—no fancy white dressed nurse to meet him.

Doctor Gilroy came out and stared at Morgan a moment, not recognizing him. "Son, you better come in here and let me look at that wound. How did you get it?"

In the back room Morgan caught the doctor's hand as he started to unwrap the cloth.

"Doc, sorry I missed breakfast this morning with you and Carl Dunnington."

The medic looked puzzled, then grinned. "Morgan, that you? Half the men in town got a gun sighted in on you."

"They got to find me first. You learn anything about how the fat man operates?"

"Not a lot. There's a ramp up the back for his chair to get it up to the second floor. He doesn't walk much any more. Gets wheeled around in this big padded chair. I guess he hasn't been on the street here for at least a year."

The medic looked closer at the bandage. "There's no hurt under that at all?"

"No, but you can look at my arm." Morgan peeled back his shirt-sleeve to reveal the tightly wrapped bandage around his upper left arm.

"Bullet graze."

The doctor treated it with some antiseptic, more salve and a fresh bandage.

"Carl found out the territorial governor will be in town on Friday. Nobody seems to know much about it, but he's a close friend of Gunther Johnson. If it's business, it must be funny business of some sort. Johnson never gets involved with projects or people unless he can make a fortune off each one."

"How is your group coming along?"

"So far we have six men, all solid and true. All have been hurt by Johnson except me. Most of them want to get an inch thick rope and hang Johnson from that big pine tree at the edge of town. We're not sure the branch is strong enough."

"They want to, but they won't?"

"That's about the reading on it. We have the other lawyer in town involved, so we are ready to step in and take legal action against Johnson and Halstead and their property if somebody breaks his power base first. We're hoping that will be you."

"Right now I'm trying to stay alive."

"Good plan. Don't get any more of these head injuries." He looked at the blood. "That real blood?"

"Catsup, doc. Has a real good taste to it."

They both chuckled.

"A man is coming in town today who might be able to help us. He should be on the afternoon stage out of Denver. If we're lucky, we might have something that will blast Johnson right off his second floor office."

Doc Gilroy looked up. "What could that be?"

"I'm not sure myself, but it has something to do with a dead woman and a small girl and some drawings and specifications."

"Some big project for here in town?"

"I'm not sure if it's for here or Denver or San Francisco. Tonight sometime we should know what's happening and figure out some way to set the matter straight."

"Good. You keep in touch with us. Carl is worried about you. Stop down there if you can. That bandage disguises you so well your own mother wouldn't recognize you."

They shook hands. Morgan rolled down his sleeve and buttoned it and walked out of the office. It was a little after one o'clock. He walked out of town, found a shaded spot under some trees and unbuttoned his shirt. He took out the heavy package and began on page one, reading the notes and trying to make sense out of the drawings. They were levels of some kind with lines that slanted upward. The next page might have the lines moving upward a little or even downward in some places.

The sets of figures meant nothing to him. Many had percentage signs after them. The plans and designs and figures were like nothing he had ever seen before.

He worked over them for an hour but knew absolutely no more than he had when he started. Something to do with engineering, but that was as far as he could get. He checked his watch—two o'clock. He had another hour. Morgan leaned back against a tree and thought about Piper. She was the daughter of the enemy. She was so young and tender and shy and lovely and totally desirable—not at all like the sexy Kristen.

For a moment his eyes closed, and when he opened them he realized he had been sleeping. He checked the watch again, buttoned the package safely inside his shirt and hurried toward town. He didn't want to be late at the small café.

When he walked inside, he left on his hat and the glasses. She was in the back booth already, and she frowned when she saw him. He could tell she recognized him.

"You've been hurt!" she said, a note of concern

showing.

"It's nothing, just a precaution. I didn't want to be late to see you."

"Good. I came early so I wouldn't miss you." She looked down, as if suddenly shy that she had made such an admission. "Are you sure you're not wounded?"

"No, I'm fine. Why are there so many men running around town with guns at the ready?"

"Oh, I don't know. Some outlaw is in town I think. That doesn't worry me." She looked up as the waitress came.

"How is your apple pie today?" Morgan asked. "Let's try two pieces and coffee."

Piper looked at him and smiled, then looked away. She touched her hair, looked at the wall, then at the clock on the wall.

"I've never done anything like this before—meet somebody for coffee who I almost don't know. Probably I shouldn't have, but I told my father about you. He's overprotective of me. He said he wanted to meet you, so I asked him to be here at three today. He's a little late."

She looked toward the front of the cafe. When she turned back she was smiling.

"Good. Here he comes now. My father is Burel Halstead. He's promised to be extremely cordial."

Morgan saw Halstead coming toward him. There was no where to run, nothing to do but face the man. He wondered if Halstead would recognize Lee Morgan behind his thin disguise?

Chapter Eight

Morgan stood up automatically as the small man with thinning hair stopped in front of their booth. Partly Morgan was being polite, but also he would be in a position to draw quickly if he had to. The older man wore a dark business suit with vest and gold watch.

Piper smiled as she looked at her father. "Daddy, I'd like to introduce you to Judson Jones. He's a businessman looking for a new store here, like I told you. Mr. Jones, this is my father, Burel Halstead."

They shook hands.

"Well, young man, it's interesting to meet you, although with that bandage I'm not sure just what you look like. Is it a bad injury?"

"No, not bad at all. The nurse was a little ambitious as she put on the bandage. She may have been playing a joke on me."

Halstead frowned as he stared at Morgan. "Well, when it comes to stopping blood flow, it doesn't hurt to go a little bit too far with the bandages."

"Sit down, Daddy. Do you want some apple pie. It's really quite good."

"Well, I really shouldn't. I have work to do." He shrugged. "It will still be there when I get back." He signaled to the waitress and ordered pie and coffee.

Halstead looked at Morgan who had sat down again.

"So, I hear you're looking for a possible store to open?"

"That's right. Some inheritance from my father's estate. I'm in no rush to start a business. First I want to find the best spot and the best kind of business for that area."

"Yes, good planning. No sense in opening another livery stable say, when there's only business enough for one. Do you think Lafayette could support a good men's haberdashery store?"

"Your daughter and I spoke of that yesterday. I'd have to check and see what kind of clothes most of the better dressed men in town wore. From my first impression there wouldn't be enough business unless the store also catered to the more expensive women's finery as well."

Halstead had a bite of his pie and nodded. "Yes, yes, I've seen such stores—men's wear on one side and women's on the other. I believe there are one or two in Denver. Of course now I have to go into Denver itself to find the proper kind of clothes."

"Understandable, Mr. Halstead. I've found that the more casual I dress, the easier it is for me to do my investigations of small towns and their business potential. If I came in wearing a thirty dollar suit with a diamond stick pin and a fifteen dollar pair of shoes, I'd be marked as a swell right off and wouldn't be able to do the kind of investigating that I need to. I have the cash in the bank for my store, but it has to be a sure thing before I'll write a draft to get started."

Halstead nodded, looked at his daughter and winked. "Well, Piper, I've had my pie for the week and met this nice young man. Now I do have to rush off. Business, more business. I mentioned that I'd be at a dinner meeting tonight with the Governor. Please tell Lotta that I won't be home until late."

Piper smiled and touched her father's shoulder as he slid out of the booth. Morgan stood up as the other man did. They shook hands, and Halstead hurried away.

Morgan sat back down and frowned. "I thought you said you did hosting duties for your father and that your mother died some time ago."

"Yes, right. My father remarried, but Lotta wouldn't have anything to do with fancy parties. She says she gets embarrassed because she doesn't know what to talk about and people make her think that she's dumb. Dumb but pretty is the way she puts it."

"Is she?"

Piper giggled. "Mr. Jones, I'm sure that you don't expect me to answer a question like that about my stepmother. Actually she's more like a sister to me. She's only twenty-two years old. Most of the town was shocked when Daddy married her. He brought her back from Denver after one of his trips. I must admit that Daddy seems pleased and happy with the marriage.

"Just so he doesn't die of a heart attack."

Piper giggled again. "Mr. Jones, what a naughty thing for you to say. I have no idea whatever you're talking about. Now we should change the subject."

They talked about the country, how pleasant it was in the summer and how trying it could be in the winter with the snow. Soon she looked at the clock on the wall.

"Goodness, I do have to hurry. I'm to be at the new library at four, and it's almost that time now."

He stood when she did, caught her hand and shook it firmly. He wanted to pull her into his arms and kiss her, but he knew that wasn't the right thing to do—at least not now and not here. He waved to her, finished his coffee, paid the bill and left.

He went past the bank and on a whim turned in. Kristen wasn't in her usual chair. He went to a desk to one side and cleared his throat. A thin young man with a nervous twitch in one eye looked up.

"Yes, sir?"

"I wondered if Kristen was about. She was working on a problem I had with my account."

The young man sighed and seemed distraught. He turned his head, pinched the bridge of his nose and cleared away moisture from his eyes.

"I'm sorry but Kristen seems to be missing. She came to work this morning, then went out for dinner at the café across the street and never came back. We can't find her anywhere."

Morgan stiffened. It had to be a ploy, using her to dig him out. The bait for the kill. What better bait? He thanked the upset young man and walked out of the bank. He wasted no time now, walking quickly toward Kristen's house. He came up to the back door through the alley, making sure that no one was watching.

He found what he expected tacked to the back screen door. Morgan pulled the note off and hurried away a block as he watched behind him. He saw no movement that might indicate someone had seen him take the note.

Morgan unfolded the paper.

"Morgan. We know you're in town and have seen Kristen. If you want her delicious body to be whole and without scars, come to the old Silver King mine three miles from town on the Denver road. The mine is a mile off the road at the second creek on the left that comes into the stream. Be there before dark or you can kiss Kristen good-bye—because she'll be dead."

Morgan turned and trotted toward the livery stable. He found Carl Dunnington there and showed him the letter.

"Damn them. I don't know when this is going to stop. Let me come with you. Two of us will be better than one. You have a rifle?"

Morgan saddled his horse while Dunnington rounded up two rifles and two boxes of shells.

"You know they want me dead on the trail," Morgan said.

"I know it. You're our best bet to beat them. That's why I want to keep you alive." He tossed Morgan a Spencer seven shot-repeating rifle.

"Loaded and ready to kill varmints," Dunnington said. "Let's ride."

The livery man was good on a horse. He knew where the mine was, but they turned off at the first creek instead of the second.

"Could have a half a dozen ambushes set for you up that second creek trail," Dunnington said.

They went over a ridge, then climbed one more and stopped just before they crested it. They dismounted and crawled up to the top of the second ridge.

In the next small valley they could see the old mine. It was abandoned. Smoke came from the chimney of a log cabin that looked like it had held up better than the mine buildings. There were two tunnels that must bore back into the mountain.

"Never paid out a dime in silver," Dunnington said. "Some rich guy from Denver figured there was silver in every mountain up here. He knows better now, but he's no longer rich."

Morgan checked the access to the cabin. There was plenty of pine, Douglas fir and mahogany down halfway to the cabin. Then the ground became rocky, and there were only occasional shoots of green not big enough to hide a man.

The rear of the cabin had no window while this side did. Morgan worked out his plan slowly. He needed a diversion.

"You good with that rifle?"

"Damn good."

"I want to come at them from the back. You go down to the right through the cover until you can get a good bead on the front door. Find a good log for protection. Then in exactly a half hour I want you to start sending some hot lead at that front door. It's probably log slabs and four inches thick.

"I'm the diversion."

"Right. With them shooting at your position and watching out the front, nobody should be covering the rear. If I'm lucky I can get to the back of the cabin before they know I'm there. From that point, I'll play it by ear. Do whatever works. Just be sure not to hit the girl with one of your shots.

"Chimney is smoking so they must be inside. All of them, we hope. You ready?"

Dunnington nodded. "We ride as far as we can in cover?"

Morgan said they would and both squirmed back down to their horses. Both looked at their watches.

"In a half hour it will be a quarter of five," Morgan said. Dunnington set his pocket watch and rode into the brush and down the other side.

Morgan picked his way up the slope another hundred yards, then checked the crest. It was well covered with timber and brush. He went over the top and worked down toward the cabin. When the brush began to thin, he got off his mount, tied her, took the Spencer and worked forward.

He knew the rifle was for long range work and counted on something a lot closer before it was over. Morgan moved down through the light brush and the pine trees, rushing from tree to tree. He was a little over 50 yards from the back of the cabin when he ran out of cover. Morgan checked his watch and saw he had almost ten minutes to wait.

It wasn't worth trying to crawl up on the back of the building. Before any firing started, they probably had lookouts on all four sides. That was the way Morgan would do it. He held his patience and waited.

The first sound of the rifle came from the front of the cabin two minutes early. Morgan silently thanked Carl and got ready to move. He watched the sides and back of the wood structure but saw no movement. Maybe they didn't have outside lookouts afterall. After three shots and what he guessed were two heavier sounding replies, Morgan crouched and headed for the cabin.

He made it to the back of the cabin without getting shot at. An occasional round went off in front, but nothing came his way.

He held the six-gun ready and edged toward the corner of the cabin. When he looked around he saw nothing new, just the logs of the cabin's side and a stretch of rocky land toward the front of the cabin.

He wasn't sure if anyone had fired a weapon from the cabin. Sounds were hard to track in the woods, especially at this high altitude. They were close to a mile high, well over five thousand feet. That had something to do with him being winded when he ran.

He checked the smoke which still came from the chimney. The roof of the cabin was made of split cedar shakes. He could pull loose a couple of them with no trouble. He went to the corner of the cabin where the uneven logs extended at various lengths. Using them as stepping stones, he climbed to the edge of the roof and eased on top cautiously.

He kept low on the roof and found two loose shakes without having to pry them. Morgan tried to move across the shakes without making any noise. A rifle snarled in front of the cabin, and he heard the hot lead thunk into one of the side logs of the structure.

He moved faster then, stood and placed both of the shingles over the top of the chimney and pressed down on them. The smoke stopped coming out. He waited a minute and saw that the weight of the two heavy shakes would hold in most of the smoke. It would come out of the stove or the fireplace below. Morgan edged away from the chimney, moved to the ridge of the peaked roof and waited.

Two minutes later there had been another rifle shot from out front at the cabin, but no response from inside. Now he could see smoke coming from the edge of the roof. It must be pouring out the door or windows.

Why hadn't anyone come out spitting and coughing and rubbing the smoke out of their eyes?

Morgan swore, ran to the back edge of the roof and jumped to the soft ground.

There was a good chance nobody came out because nobody was alive inside. He ran to the window on the side and tried to look inside. There was no glass in it, but a blanket had been nailed over it. He tried the window on the other side and found it open. Nothing covered it.

He could see most of the inside of the one room cabin. He spotted no one. The fire in the fireplace had nearly burned out. Large logs had been used on top of smaller ones. He bellowed a challenge through the window and ducked. There was no response.

He ran to the front of the cabin and held his rifle over his head.

"Don't shoot!" he brayed into the cover in front of the cabin. Morgan ran to the front door of the cabin and saw there was no latch or lock. He kicked it open and darted through, six-gun in hand.

It was as he had feared. No one was there, only a room full of smoke. A note on white paper with the same block lettering was on the kitchen table. He picked it up, hurried out of the thick smoke and read it.

"Nice try. Now follow directions. Go back to the main Denver road and ride two miles west. Take the lane marked, Mauser. Follow it to the end. Maybe the girl will be there, and maybe that's where you'll die!"

Morgan called to Dunnington and told him to wait where he was. Morgan took off at a run to where he had left his horse. He mounted and galloped back to the cabin, then onto the trail until he found Dunnington and gave him the note.

"What are they trying to do?" the livery owner asked.

"Trying to keep me out of town. Why I don't know. That part's working. If they're trying to kill me as well, that part won't work. They don't know how hard I am to kill."

They rode back to the Denver wagon track and stopped. "You don't have to come with me on this next run," Morgan said.

Dunnington shrugged. "In for a penny . . ."

They rode.

This time they waited for the road mentioned on the note and turned off. Morgan told Dunnington to stay a quarter of a mile behind him. That way he could be a backup in case Morgan got in trouble.

"I just can't figure out what to expect. They'll know I'm coming. That makes it harder. Going to be dark before I get there."

Morgan rode around a small bend in the road, stepped down from the horse and walked the animal down the road. When he gave it a whack with his hand, the horse moved on down the road at a trot, then at a walk.

Morgan vanished into the brush and trees at the side of the trail and ran forward, keeping up with the horse. Twice he had to run into the road and slap the horse forward. The last time the animal stopped, Morgan threw small rocks at her to get her in motion. At last she must have smelled water, because the mare stepped out briskly. It was heavy dusk now. The sound of the horse came through plainly, but to the eyes she was only a ghostly shadow moving forward.

Morgan ran through the woods at the side of the road. His first reaction came when he saw lights ahead of what could be a house or cabin.

The horse walked forward eagerly now. It was 40 yards from the lights in the house when two shotguns cut loose. One was on each side of the trail, and each fired two rounds. The horse screamed in pain and went down.

Morgan moved up closer now in the full darkness. He saw two men bending over the horse. He was only 30 feet away when one of the men lit a match and held it up.

Morgan shot both of them dead with his six-gun. They went down without a sound.

He ran lightly past them toward the house. Morgan chose a back window and looked in. He could see nothing. He moved to the next window that must be in a living room. By the light from two lamps he could see Kristen bound to a chair. Her blouse was off, and her breasts showed plainly.

Morgan tried to check the rest of the room, but he could only see part of it. He waited.

"Won't be long now," a heavy voice said. "I want to see Morgan's head in that bucket." The words came through muffled and soft. Morgan moved around toward the front steps. He went up the steps with a heavy tread and walked across the six-foot wide porch. He swung open the door with his left hand.

"Tex, that you?" the same gruff, heavy voice from inside asked. "Come in here with that bucket. I want to see this Morgan guy's head."

Morgan stormed in fast. The big man with the heavy voice stared at him a minute, then Morgan's Colt barked and the man's right kneecap shattered as he dropped to the floor, screaming in pain.

Morgan walked up and shot him in the shoulder joint so nothing could ever make his arm work right again.

He kicked a six-gun away from the downed man, then hurried to Kristen and untied her and helped her into her blouse.

"Only three of them?" he asked her.

She nodded.

Morgan went back to the man writhing on the floor.

"So you'd like to see my head, would you? Take a look. You'll remember it all the way to hell."

Morgan made sure the killer saw him, then shot him through his screaming mouth.

It took Morgan ten minutes to find the horses, get them saddled and ride for town. They found Dunnington back a quarter of a mile.

"When I heard them shotguns go off I figured you'd paid the price in full and settled up," Dunnington said. "Ain't nobody who can get away from four shotgun loads especially if they're double aught buck loads."

Morgan told him what he did.

"How did you know?"

"Seen that trick more than once. A man lives long enough, he learns these little things."

Kristen said the men hadn't touched her except to take her blouse off. They were holding off on the party until after they killed Morgan. Then they all three would celebrate with Kristen as long as they could get it up.

"I owe you, Lee Morgan," Kristen said. "I owe you my life. They never would have let me live with what I knew they were going to do."

"Hell is gonna be full, Morgan, if you hang around Lafayette much longer," Dunnington said.

"Couldn't happen to more deserving men," Morgan said. They rode a while.

"When did you say the Governor was getting into town?"

"Supposed to be there about five this afternoon. About the time we got to that first cabin."

"Any idea why he's coming?"

"Somebody said it was to make an inspection trip for his report to the government on progress the territory is making."

Morgan snorted. "Sounds like a waste of time report."

Morgan tried to think of what else was bothering him, but it escaped him. He turned to the livery man. "Carl, you know anything about civil engineering?"

"Not much. I was on the city council for a while. We talked about putting in a water system. They said we'd need to get a civil engineer out of Denver to plan it out and layout where the pipes were going and establish a reservoir back up one of the creeks. The engineers asking price per day was about what we had in the whole damn city treasury at the time."

"Who else uses them?"

"Hard rock mines that go deep have them, but they call them mining engineers. Lay out the tunnels and air shafts and all that. Some towns use them to lay out the plots for the town and the streets and all."

Morgan snapped his fingers. "Let's see if these horses can move faster. I just remembered why the Governor is coming."

Chapter Nine

Kristen and Dunnington both looked at Morgan in the pale moonlight.

"You remembered why the Governor is coming to town?" Kristen asked.

"Well, not so much why as who. Today Burel Halstead said he had to meet the Governor tonight."

"He told you that?" Dunnington asked.

"Not exactly. He told his daughter, and I happened to overhear him. If Halstead is meeting with the Governor, you can bet that Johnson is meeting him, too. Now what are those three cooking up, and how does it affect this small town?"

They all rode faster.

It was well after seven o'clock when they got back to town, put the horses in the livery and stood across the street staring at the light in the offices over the hardware store where Gunther Johnson lived.

Morgan had taken the bandages off his face once he and Dunnington had started riding out of town that afternoon, but now for a moment he wished that he had them back. It was strange standing there looking at the windows where his enemies were and not being able to do anything about it.

"We need to go see Mrs. Miller," he said. They followed him down the street and around to the back of the Miller General Store. It was locked. Morgan knocked loud and long, waited, then knocked again with the butt of his six-gun.

A minute later a voice came through the rear door.

"What do you want?"

"Mrs. Miller, it's me, Lee Morgan. Did that man come from New Mexico?"

He heard the bolt slide back, and the small door opened. Mrs. Miller waved them all in and nodded at the other two.

"They both are on our side. Don't worry about them. Did Woo get here?"

"He did. He's here and wants to see you."

"Good. Did the Governor come into town?"

"He did—in an expensive coach that us taxpayers are furnishing him with. He should have to ride the stage like the rest of us."

"Where is he?"

"He took the entire third floor at the hotel. He's having some meeting there tonight from what I hear. Fred came in and got a fancy new lock to put on the Governor's door for tonight. Said the one there could be opened with a hairpin."

Morgan turned to Dunnington. "Thanks for the help today. I better talk to this man alone. It could be the end of all of our problems or the start of some new ones. Breakfast in the morning at the usual spot?"

Dunnington nodded and stepped outside. Mrs. Miller looked at Kristen.

"Johnson and his henchmen kidnapped Kristen this afternoon and took her to a cabin. They left me a note to get me to come rescue her."

"Looks like you did," Mrs. Miller said. "They tried to kill you when you went for her, right?"

Morgan nodded. "Honey, you can stay here until the meeting is over, then I bet Morgan will volunteer to walk you home. He's a little dense, but he ain't that stupid."

Morgan pretended to punch her in the shoulder.

"Come on into the living room. If you're lucky, Kristen, you can meet my little girl, Lisa."

Lisa liked Kristen at first sight, and the two settled down on the couch and began reading books to each other.

Two minutes later, Mrs. Miller knocked on an upstairs door and a small Chinese man opened it and bowed.

"Ah, this must be Mr. Morgan I hear so much about. Miller lady talk about Mr. Morgan all time."

Morgan bowed slightly. "Yes, I'm Morgan. Would now be a good time to talk?"

"I come three hundred miles bumping all over coach. Now best time to talk."

The three of them went inside, and Morgan watched the small Oriental. How was he supposed to read this man? He showed no emotion at all.

He plunged right in. "Mr. Woo, I happened upon a dying woman and her little girl. The woman

said her name was Bernice Upton and she was
the daughter of Keefe Upton and they all used
to live here in Lafayette. Mr. Upton worked for
Mr. Gunther Johnson. What I need to know is in
what capacity did Johnson hire Mr. Upton?"

Woo spread his hands. "I do not know. The
Uptons came to Santa Fe, and we became
acquainted. I have a store there and several
other business. I also have read for the law. I
have some documents from Mr. Upton, a will
actually, leaving all of his worldly goods to his
daughter, who you tell me now is deceased. That
is too bad."

"Did Mr. Upton have much of an estate?"
Morgan asked.

"Yes and no. A house in Santa Fe, and some
stocks that may be of no value. He said he sent
to his daughter his most valuable asset. I was
hoping that she might have given it to you to
give to me to add to the estate. It now would go
to the granddaughter, Lisa."

"She gave me no money, Mr. Woo, or stocks or
bonds or anything else of apparent value except
her small daughter, who I would guess you've
met."

"Ah, yes. Lisa."

"What kind of work did Mr. Upton do in Santa
Fe?"

"He worked for the city, trying to lay out straight
streets and blocks and to bring some order after
years of goat trails and cow paths."

"How did he manage that?"

"He was a civil engineer, a surveyor, a gifted
man with a chain and a transit and level."

"So what work could he have done for Mr.
Johnson?"

Mr. Woo shook his head. "I truly have no idea. He did not lay out the town in lots and streets. He must not have worked for a mining company establishing its tunnels. He told me once he had never been underground in a mine."

"Mr. Woo, are you by any chance also an engineer?"

The Chinese man shook his head. "No, I did not have that much education before I left China, and here I had trouble enough to learn English."

"You have done remarkably well, Mr. Woo."

"Mr. Woo is going to write up legal papers so I can be named the legal guardian of Lisa," Mrs. Miller said. "He said it's only a formality if the paper work is right. He'll do that tomorrow. We won't file the papers until this problem about the Uptons is all settled and over with."

Morgan nodded. Now the girl's future was assured. He had only to hand over the papers in his shirt and be done with the whole thing. However, he hesitated. Something didn't feel quite right.

"Do you know Mr. Johnson, Mr. Woo?"

"Only from what Mr. Upton told me. Not a good man if I understand the talk from Mr. Upton."

"That's putting it mildly. He's a petty despot trying to run the whole county, and now evidently he has a strong tie with the Governor."

"That would be bad."

"Mr. Woo, would you try to think again about your talks with Mr. Upton. Surely he told you what kind of work or what project he did for Mr. Johnson. The two of them must have argued about it, and then Mr. Upton left town before Mr. Johnson's men could find him."

Mr. Woo rubbed his chin and looked at the ceiling. A moment later he nodded. "Now thinking more, he did say two or three times that he worked on the line. That's all I remember him saying. He didn't agree with Mr. Johnson about the line."

Morgan scowled. "Line, the line. That could be a property line, the state line, the territorial line, the continental divide line that runs through the Rocky Mountains. The line. It doesn't make much sense, does it? A surveyor would be concerned with property lines, but I can't make anything of that."

Morgan thought more about it. Nothing made sense.

"What about the stage line?" Mrs. Miller asked.

"That's another line, but it still doesn't figure. Why would Johnson have Mr. Upton engineering a stage line? We already have one through to Denver."

"I am sorry, but that's all I know," Mr. Woo said. "I hoped that you might have something for me of value for the estate."

Mrs. Miller looked at Morgan and shook her head. It was a small movement, but Morgan saw it.

"Wish we did, Mr. Woo. That little girl Lisa is worth more than any amount of gold or silver you could dig out of these mountains, but she can't show up on a ledger sheet."

"Mr. Woo, I know that you've had a long journey," Mrs. Miller said. "Tomorrow when you're rested, we'll talk again and get the papers filled out for Lisa to be the heir and have me named as her legal guardian."

"Some rest would be most appreciated. I am not as young as I once was."

They said good night and went down to the first floor.

Mrs. Miller boiled some coffee and took out some cinnamon rolls.

"Could Woo be in on this with Johnson?" Morgan asked.

"Don't see how. He's been in Santa Fe."

"Letters could have been sent from Santa Fe without a return," Morgan said. "You see any come through for Johnson?"

"He gets so much mail I never would have noticed anything like that. Why would I watch?"

"So he could have mailed some information to Johnson, come here hoping to get whatever the package is and then turn it over to Johnson for a small cut of its value."

"You believe that about Upton being a civil engineer and doing something about a line?" Mrs. Miller asked.

"Sounds reasonable. The package is filled with some kind of engineering data and reports and forms. We know that."

Kristen was still reading and talking with Lisa who was getting sleepy.

Morgan pounded the table with his fist. "There has to be some way to find out what Johnson is up to. He has taken the whole top floor of the hotel. No easy way to eavesdrop on him."

"We could follow Woo tomorrow?"

"Easy enough, but is there anything we can do tonight?" Morgan asked, not expecting an answer.

Mrs. Miller shook her head and stood up. "At least nothing that I can do tonight." She looked at Morgan and then at Kristen who was now holding a sleeping Lisa. "Go ahead, and walk her home. I'll see you tomorrow."

*   *   *

Ten minutes later he and Kristen went in her house through the unlocked back door. No one had been waiting for them. Morgan locked the doors and windows, then sat down on the bed.

Kristen did a slow striptease as he sat there. When she was nude she eased down on his lap and kissed him.

"Morgan, I owe you my life, you know that? I'll never forget it. Anything I have, anything I am, is all yours. I owe you so much I can't even think up enough good things to do for you to even start to repay you. I'll try to make that start right now."

She moved off his lap, unbuckled his belt and then opened his pants. She found his penis and quickly brought it to life. One hand caught his heavy sack and gently massaged his balls.

"Kristen, you don't have to."

"I know. That's what makes it even more exciting for me. I've never done a man this way, not all the way. I want to now."

She lowered her head and kissed the tip of his throbbing penis, then opened her lips and pushed down over his lance.

"Oh, damn," Morgan said softly. He pushed her down on the bed and lay on his side. Her lips slid around him again, and he began a gentle thrusting into her mouth. His hands reached down, found her bare breasts and fondled them.

Slowly he picked up the pace of his sideways humping. It was strange, different, wild.

He stopped.

She looked up at him.

"Kristen, are you sure?"

She bobbed her head and went back to work on him, furnishing the up and down motion until he moaned softly and continued to thrust his hips forward cautiously. Morgan felt the mounting pressure. He'd been serviced this way before, but not by such a delicious young woman. He visualized her again when she had been on her hands and knees with her breasts hanging down like two upside-down volcanos. Then she had shifted her round little bottom toward him.

Morgan gave a soft cry, his breath came in gasps and he thrust harder and harder, faster and faster. He exploded in her with a wild moan, thrust twice more, then eased back. She came off him smiling and cuddled against his chest while he caught his breath.

It was five minutes later before he reached for her breasts.

"Sweet, generous, marvelous Kristen. Any debt you thought you might have had to me is paid in full. No more payments required."

She stared at him, then smiled and kissed his lips softly. "If you say so, Lee Morgan. Whatever you say."

"We better get some sleep. I don't know what's going to happen tomorrow." He undressed and slid between the sheets. She lay there in the darkness watching him.

"Lee Morgan, I am yours now and forever, but I will never do anything you don't want me to do. Say the word and I'll be with you or let you go alone. Whatever you wish, I will do." She bent and kissed his cheek, then lay down beside him.

Morgan frowned for a moment. This woman could be a problem. He lifted his brows as he thought about it. If she would do what he wanted, then there would be no problem. He'd have to see how it worked out.

He listened as she went to sleep at once.

Morgan lay there trying to think it through. Was Woo on their side, or was he working with Johnson? What was Johnson up to that the Governor would be in on? More to the point right now, how did he find out what the package was without tipping his hand to Johnson? Morgan turned over three times before he went to sleep.

Once during the night he awoke to find Kristen pressed against him with one hand wrapped round his chest.

At once Morgan decided he liked it and drifted back to sleep.

Chapter Ten

That same night in rooms 303 and 304 of the Princess Hotel, Territorial Governor Alonzo Kennedy, Gunther Johnson and Burel Halstead sat around a low table in a room that had quickly been converted from a bedroom into a living room with a sofa, two big chairs and a low table in the center.

"Those plans are somewhere," Governor Kennedy stormed. He walked to the window, then marched to the door and back to the soft chair which he sank into scowling. "Why the hell haven't you found them? Upton took off from here with them. I warned you not to trust him completely."

"He was watched," Johnson said with a touch of a whine. "He was simply gone before we knew he was that unhappy."

"Money. Money usually keeps people like him happy. You traced him to Santa Fe and missed him there, then the papers vanished and you think his daughter had them. If so why didn't your man find them when he searched her and her gear at that cabin?"

"I don't know, Governor. The only lead we have is this man, Morgan, who seems to be as slippery as a trout in a greased glove."

"For heaven sakes don't kill him until we find out if he has the papers. That would be the last mistake you ever made for me, Johnson. Just where is this Morgan now?"

Gunther Johnson wiped his brow with his handkerchief. It had taken him over an hour to be lifted and pushed and carried and badgered to walk from his chair into the hotel and up the three flights of steps. He was so exhausted he could hardly breathe, let alone think. He had sent three men with the girl to try to trap Morgan. Their instructions were to kill him if they had to. He sweat some more.

"Morgan. Yes, he's in town somewhere, but he isn't staying at the hotel. Perhaps in the woods in back of town."

The governor tipped a bottle of cold beer that an aide provided him. "Be damn sure we talk to him tomorrow. You know that next week the United States Congress takes up the matter. We must be ready to show them that the line is practical and that we can build it. For that we need all of the specifications."

"Most of which are in that notebook that Upton kept," Halstead said. "I knew we should have had him make two copies of all of his reports."

"A little late for that now, isn't it? If we can't show those papers and a summary of them to Congress, we can kiss this project right out the old window. I've been working on this for three years, gentlemen. It's far too late now to get a setback like this."

"Perhaps a postponement of the hearings by the Congressional committee?" Halstead ventured. "I'll be glad to write the wires and then go to Washington D.C. by train and reason with them. Engineering projects like this one are difficult at best, and these men realize that. I can say that our engineering plans aren't quite finished yet."

"That would be a last resort. I've promised these men twice now that we would make their deadline. They have been suckered on too many fake deals like this before to get caught again. Which means we must have finished engineering specifications."

"Which we have—they are just misplaced," Johnson said. He mopped his face with his handkerchief, then dropped that one on the floor and took a fresh one from his pocket. He never used a handkerchief twice.

"Remember, Gunther, all of those parcels of land you bought will be worth damn little if this deal doesn't go through. I hope you don't owe a lot of money on that twelve mile stretch you bought."

Johnson turned and stared at the Governor. "How in hell did you know about that one?"

"I have eyes and ears everywhere. How do you think that I knew you didn't have those engineering papers yet?"

The Governor stood and paced again. An aide handed him an already lit cigar which he smoked and used as a pointer.

"If this deals falls through, Johnson, you and your neat little kingdom here are all through. I'll personally see that you lose every dime that you have, whether you gained it legally or not. Is that perfectly clear?"

"Yes sir, Governor," Halstead said. "Mr. Johnson and I both understand your position. We're not trying to embarrass you or to be evasive. We just don't have the damn papers!"

"Get them by noon tomorrow!"

The three men stared at each other. Halstead wavered first, then looked away. Johnson shook his head. "We're trying, Governor. Now if our business is over, I've arranged for a small bit of entertainment."

Johnson signaled, and before the Governor or his three aides could move, a line of six girls danced into the room. They were from the Bird Cage Saloon, one of the two saloons with girls upstairs that Johnson owned in town. These ladies actually did do a small dance number on a makeshift stage that was usually used for high stakes poker games.

Halstead ushered out the three staff men and closed the door.

The girls danced across in front of the men. Then one girl shrieked, and the entire top of her costume came down. Both her arms were locked in place by the other dancers in the row so she couldn't lift her costume to cover her breasts. They danced across again, the girl's big breasts bouncing and jolting with every step.

The Governor chuckled and pointed at the girl.

On the way back across the room two more of the girls' tops fell down. On the third pass all of the girls were bare to the waist and dancing up a storm. After one more bouncing pass, they all squealed and ran up and clustered around the Governor's chair.

Another squeal, and one girl fell into his lap.

"Johnson, you know how to find good entertainment," the Governor said. He reached over and tweaked the girl's nipples. She laughed and begged him to do it again.

Almost before he realized what was happening, the Governor was being undressed by the six topless dancers. They pulled his shirt off and then his pants. Two of the girls kicked out of the rest of their costumes, caught the Governor by the hand and led him through the connecting door into the bedroom.

Two more girls kicked free of their costumes and ran naked into the room, then closed the door.

The other two girls stopped performing like a switch had been thrown. They pulled up their tops and stood against the wall. Their part in the little game was over.

Johnson ignored them for a moment. How the hell was he going to get those papers if his men did kill Morgan? He motioned to one of his runners who hurried downstairs to try to find out what happened out on the Denver road.

That done, he stared at the two prostitutes still in the room.

"You want us to go back to work at the saloon, Mr. Johnson, or does Mr. Halstead here get a bonus tonight?" the taller of the two girls said.

"Hell, he ain't done nothing to deserve a bonus."

"Sometimes a bonus for a worker spurs him on to better things the next day," the same girl said. She dropped the top of her costume and in one swift movement stepped out of the rest of it.

Johnson snorted. "Hell, why not. He's trying. I'm trying. Maybe a little two-girl job will get old

Burel here to come up with ideas to trap that damn Morgan, if he ain't already dead."

The girls squealed and rushed to Halstead. They pulled him over to the couch and tore off his clothes.

Johnson sat where he was in the big overstuffed chair and stared at the spectacle.

Halstead grabbed at his pants. "Hey, Gunther, you gonna leave?"

"Hell, no, I'm gonna watch. Check up on these employees and see if they can still do a good job. That one there's got tits that are starting to sag."

She stuck her tongue out at Johnson, giggled and pulled Halstead's pants and underwear off, leaving him naked and squirming on the couch.

One of the girls pushed his head down on a pillow, then straddled him and lowered her crotch straight at his mouth.

"Great lord!" he wailed, then grabbed her and pulled her to him, his tongue and mouth working fast.

The other girl concentrated on his privates. She had him rock hard in two minutes, then played with him until he wailed. She teased him and enticed him until his hips began to pump up and down from where he lay on his back. She knew the signs. She lathered his penis with her saliva, then positioned herself over his hips and straddled him, lowering gently as his member penetrated and slanted all the way into her.

A moment later, Halstead bellowed in a kind of victory cheer as he humped upward a dozen times and brayed as he pushed the girl away from his face and stared at the second naked girl he had penetrated.

"God damn!" Halstead whispered—then he passed out.

The girls were gone when Halstead came back to consciousness. Four helpers were working with Johnson moving him out of the room and toward the hall. Halstead found that the girls had dressed him before they left. He must really have been out.

He watched the men helping the huge body of Gunther Johnson move down the hall. If they dropped him and he fell down the steps it might crush the entire staircase.

Halstead didn't worry about Johnson for long. Where in hell was that guy Morgan, and if he was still alive, how could they tear those engineering papers away from him? Without those specifications, their whole plan could evaporate like an early morning mist in the sunlight.

He thought about the wild time with the two girls and decided this would be a day to remember no matter what happened to their big project. He hoped after having four girls with him all night that the Governor would be in a better mood in the morning. The Congressmen could be bought, and the plan could be postponed. Hell, they could hire another engineer to redo everything. All was not lost.

Gunther Johnson was exhausted and nearly passed out by the time his four men got him to the bottom of the third flight of steps. He had played the Governor about right. He knew that the four girls would delight him so much he might forget to be mad the next morning.

The man he had sent to check on Morgan came back with disquieting information. Morgan, the girl and someone else had ridden into town less than two hours before. They left horses at the livery and vanished into the darkness.

Good, the bastard was still alive. Where would he stay the night? At the general store? Probably not. At the girl's house? That would be too obvious. Probably at some small camp along the river a half mile out of town. That would be the smartest way.

His man at the stage company had left an envelope for him. He opened it and read the note.

"A Chinese man arrived on the late afternoon stage from Denver. His name is Woo Fan Too. He is from Santa Fe, New Mexico Territory. At last report he was met by Mrs. Miller of the general store. There's a chance he is staying there tonight."

Johnson smiled and nodded. Yes, yes, this might not have been such a bad day after all. The Chinaman was in town. Things might be looking up.

Johnson called in a pair of men and talked to them quietly. It was not yet ten o'clock. The two men nodded and left. A few minutes later they found the window in the alley they sought and made sure it was the right one.

One of the men stood on a wooden box and broke the window, then waited. He heard no one from inside or outside. He reached in and unlatched the window, lifted it and slipped through the opening into the Miller General Store's back room.

Moments later the inside man opened the rear door, and the second man went in. They moved quietly searching the rooms on the ground floor behind the store. They found the older woman and a child.

The smaller man located the stairs, and they went up as quietly as they could. At the top were two rooms, both bedrooms. One was empty. They drew their guns and opened the door without a sound.

Woo Fan Too sat up in bed and turned up the lamp that he had left on low. He stared at the two men, then bowed.

"You must be from Johnson. You are clumsy, make too much noise—and you are late. I expected to hear from Mr. Johnson sometime earlier than this."

The Chinaman had not taken off his clothes. He stood and made a mess of the bed, then tipped over his suitcase spilling most of the contents on the floor. He upset the chair quietly and put the second lamp on the floor and tipped it over. Then he blew out the lamp.

"Now, we go down the steps quietly. One of you hold my arm in case the woman wakes up. At the back door I'll scream and you fire two shots into the ceiling. Then we go out the door and run like a dragon is chasing us."

The two hired guns grinned in the dark. They must have thought this was the easiest job they had ever done for Mr. Johnson.

At the back door, they paused. Woo Fan Too opened the door and let some moonlight filter in. He pointed to one man's weapon which he took out and pointed at the ceiling.

Woo Fan Too screeched out a terrible cry and then screamed again as if his life were about to end. Over the last of it the man fired his six-gun twice. Then the three dashed out the door, left it open and ran to the near end of the block and down to Main Street.

They hurried into the alley behind Main and went up the ramp to the rear entrance to Gunther Johnson's kingdom.

Once inside, Woo shook hands with both of his captors and was taken in to see Johnson. The big man had changed clothes and wore only a loosely draped gown of thin silk that was both cool and pleasing on his skin.

"Ah, so, the venerable Chinese man from Santa Fe. I trust you had a good trip?"

"Why did you wait so long to contact me?" Woo Fan Too said sharply. It was more of a challenge than a question. "We have much at stake here and you sit around and talk nonsense with the Governor."

One of the guards who stood beside Johnson's chair stepped forward toward Woo, but Johnson held up his hand.

"This is no time for anger among us. It is a big project, and there will be many benefits for all. First we need the papers, the plans and specifications that Mr. Upton worked out. Did the drifter, Morgan, have them?"

"If he did, I failed to get them. I had a feeling he might not have complete trust in me."

"But does he have them?"

Woo stared at the fat man. He wanted to shudder in horror but knew that he should not. Slowly he shook his head. "I am not sure. He may. If he has them he has no idea what they are or how important they are."

"Are you sure, Chinaman?"

"I am sure. I am a student of human nature. The young man is a white knight in armor, searching to find the right thing to do with the holy grail he has in his hands. He's confused, but not stupid.

Don't underestimate him."

"I've done that twice. I won't again. The Governor is here and furious that we don't have the plans. Where is Morgan?"

"Not at the store. My guess is he is with a woman. He is the type."

"That would be Kristen. He's the key. We should take him alive tonight while he has to worry about protecting the woman. Yes, a good plan. I can send five good men."

"Go in quietly, take the man, kill the woman and burn down the house," Woo said. "Fire is the great equalizer and cleanser."

"Why burn it? I own the house."

Woo Fan Too shook his head sadly. "Confucius says there is no right way to do a wrong thing. Woo Fan Too says there always is a right way to do a wrong thing if you think it through long enough. Kill the woman, this Morgan will be incensed, forget his caution, and in his rage he will reveal where he has hidden the engineering plans."

Johnson chuckled. "Chinaman, you do have a style about you. A gift. Do you want to go along and lead my men? They will do exactly what you tell them. Oh, for fire I'd suggest a gallon or two of coal oil spread around the house. Makes it burn faster without any chance a bucket brigade could put it out. Do you have a weapon?"

Woo turned quickly, his long black braid down his back swinging with him. A moment later he had a derringer in one hand and a long, slightly curved knife in the other, both pointing precisely at the fat man's heart.

"Lord in a bucket. Looks like you do have a weapon. Let me call in some men and you can take your pick."

*   *   *

In the small house Kristen rented from the real estate firm, Lee Morgan turned over. He was awake. Unusual. He didn't wake up during the night unless something roused him. He swung his feet over the bed and pulled on his pants. His boots went on and then his gunbelt. He edged toward the door.

Behind him he heard the woman stir, then quiet.

Something was wrong, Morgan knew. Someone was in the other room. He had misjudged Johnson. He didn't think the fat man would come after him here tonight. Morgan looked at the window. It would make too much noise. He cocked his six-gun and swung around, flat against the wall. Just then the bedroom door blasted open as someone kicked it. Two bodies slammed into the room with their guns glinting in the soft light from the window.

Chapter Eleven

Lee Buckskin Morgan shot the first man who charged into the room in the chest and clubbed the second one with his six-gun as he swung in Morgan's direction.

He watched the first man in the faint light. He lifted one hand, then dropped it as a long gush of air came from his lungs. The man Morgan had hit with his six-gun started to recover. Morgan pushed his boot down on the man's throat just enough so he could breathe only with difficulty.

Morgan tried to hear if there was anyone else in the small house. He figured there was. Were they after him or the girl—or both?

He moved his foot off the man on the floor and kicked him in the head, dumping him into unconsciousness.

Morgan stepped toward the bedroom door. Somewhere in the small house he sensed someone else—just who he wasn't sure. The man moved like a cat, intent on leaving. The briefest of shadows crossed the living room heading for the front door which remained open.

When the shadow came in front of the square of light from the front door, Morgan fired. The man screamed, leaped outside and ran. Morgan rushed to the front door, but the figure vanished in the darkness.

Back in the bedroom, Morgan comforted Kristen. "It's all right. There were just three of them and they are taken care of. I want to talk to this one." He grabbed the unconscious man and dragged him to the kitchen.

Morgan took a cupful of water from the pail near the inside pump and threw the water in the man's face. He spluttered and groaned, then his eyes blinked open.

Kristen had lit a lamp and brought it into the kitchen. Morgan stared at the man. He hadn't seen him before.

"What's your name?" Morgan demanded.

"Nance," the man said.

"How many of you were there?"

"Four. One guy stayed outside."

"Who was outside?"

"The Chink, the guy with a long black braid down his back."

"Woo Fan Too?"

"Yeah, I guess. Only Chink in town."

"Who sent you?"

"Can't tell you."

"Your buddy in the bedroom is dead. You want to tell him?"

The man's eyes went wide, as he wiped water off his face. "Damn, they'll kill me sure if I tell you."

"Not if you're on a horse riding for Denver. Who sent you?"

"Johnson. Lawyer guy Halstead hired us. We just been in town two days. What the hell's going on here, a war?"

"About right. Come on, we're going for a walk." Morgan helped him stand and led him to the front door. He drew his six-gun that now had six rounds in it and pointed the man out the front door.

"Go ahead. You're free to go. Just walk outside."

"You're truth speaking?

"God's own truth. Get moving before I change my mind."

Morgan crouched as the man pushed open the screen door and stepped out on the porch. Morgan held the screen door open with his foot, still crouching. The man got to the edge of the porch when three shots blasted from 30 feet away on the dark street.

Morgan had his Colt up waiting. He sent five fast shots in the direction of the gun flashes. He heard the man on the porch scream as he was hit. Morgan saw him fall off the porch, then he charged out the door and ran for the spot where he had seen the gun flashes. He had his weapon up with one more round in it.

When he got there he saw the weapon was not needed. Woo Fan Too lay sprawled in the dust. He still held the revolver in his hand. Two rounds had caught him in the chest, and he was no longer worried about his store or the problems in Lafayette. Morgan left him where he was.

Inside the small house, Morgan lifted the corpse from the bedroom and carried him outside. He dumped him near the Chinaman and went back to the house.

When he got inside, Kristen had dressed. She had on shoes and a dress and a sweater against the chill of the high country summer night. He put on his shirt, then he and Kristen took a blanket and hurried out the back door. They walked out of town, past the small stream and found a spot on a little slope where they could see all directions.

"Why didn't we stay by the creek?" Kristen asked.

"The running water makes too much noise," Morgan said. "Half a tribe of Cheyenne could sneak up on you and you'd never hear them. Up here I'll hear anything bigger than a mouse that moves within a hundred feet of us."

They spread the blanket and lay down; he held her as she went to sleep. He knew she'd seen too much death for one long day, but there was nothing he could say to help her.

Morgan lay there a long time, watching and listening. Why did they make the push on him tonight? Maybe not to kill him but to capture him. Neither of the attackers had fired as soon as they came in the room. They must have wanted to capture him. They must know for sure that he had the engineering papers.

He'd thought of one more possibility for the line. Denver didn't have a telegraph line yet. There was a connection to make between Denver and Cheyenne which would tap them into the transcontinental telegraph that had been completed across the country in 1861. It would get Denver on the map. That could be the line they were talking about—the route for a telegraph line to Denver.

Morgan didn't worry about the Chinaman. He'd been playing both ends against the middle, trying to make sure that he was on the winning side. Turned out he came up on the losing side.

Morgan thought about breakfast. He and Kristen would both show up, and he'd go in without any disguise. If the headhunters wanted to try him, he'd call them out on the street. He was getting tired of messing around with Johnson. He was getting closer and closer to a one-on-one confrontation with the fat man. He finally had figured out how to get into the man's second floor fortress. He just didn't know exactly when he'd make his move.

Kristen woke up about three in the morning, reaching for him and sobbing. He put his arms around her and held her as she cried it out. When her sobbing stopped and she caught her breath in huge gasps, she turned her tear-stained face up to him.

"Did those men all really die? Three of them at that cabin and three more back there at my house?"

"Yes, they were trying to kill us. It was a matter of them or us. This time it happened to be them. They were not good people. They hired out as killers and rapists."

"I know." She sobbed again to catch her breath. "But they were human beings. None of us are all good."

He kissed her cheek. "You get some sleep now, and we'll talk about it in the morning. I'm taking you out to breakfast."

"Do you think . . . do you think that Mr. Johnson will send more men to try to . . . to kill us?"

"Not in broad daylight. He still wants to keep his image of being an ordinary businessman. Unless he's really desperate, we should be safe enough during the day."

"Those plans, those engineering plans are what they want, right?"

"Yes."

"Why don't we just give them to Johnson and take the stage to Denver and be rid of all of this shooting and killing."

"Because it wouldn't stop. I think those plans are valuable and that Johnson stole them from Mr. Upton in the first place, or tried to, and now I want their true value established and that amount of money given to little Lisa Upton to insure her future."

Kristen took a long breath and let it out slowly. "Morgan, you're nothing but an old softy." She reached up and kissed his lips so lightly he barely felt it, then she snuggled down and went to sleep.

Just after six A.M., Morgan and Kristen waited across the street in the alley until the café opened. They were the first customers and went to the back booth. Five minutes later the other two men came and sat in the same booth.

They nodded at Kristen.

"She's more a part of this than either of you, so anything you say to me, she can hear. Kristen was kidnapped yesterday and last night four men tried to kill her in her bed."

Dr. Gilroy lifted his brows, and even Carl Dunnington showed surprise about the nighttime raid.

Their breakfast of hot cakes and eggs and toast and coffee came, and they all ate in silence. Morgan was the first to speak.

"What it all comes down to is a set of engineering plans that Keefe Upton made for Johnson.

He left with them, and Johnson has been doing anything he had to to get them back. What I can't figure out is what the plans are for. You two hear anything about what Johnson and the Governor might be planning?"

Dr. Gilroy held up his fork. "I heard that the Governor is thinking of going to Washington D.C. to plead some kind of a case that involves us here in Colorado Territory. But there's no hint what it might be."

"The driver of the rig that drove them from Denver brought in the horses last night. He's the talkative kind, but he didn't have much to say about why the Governor is in town. I can work on him. Maybe loosen him up with some good gin I have."

"What about a murder indictment against Johnson," Morgan asked. "He hired men to come and kill Kristen last night. Can your lawyer work that up?"

"Evidence," Dr. Gilroy said. "You don't have any but the word of a dead man. Won't work in court. We need some live witnesses."

"One man got away. There were four of them. One of them is still alive, but we'd play old Ned finding him."

"Our lawyer friend says that Johnson and Halstead are buying up land in the county north of Denver. He can't tell why. Some of it is south of town here and some north. We can't figure out why either."

Morgan frowned. "Buying land. Where is it, all over or in one long strip?"

"He didn't say, but we can sure find out at the county clerk's office."

"Don't let your man ask about those specific

properties. We don't want word getting back to Johnson."

"I know the county clerk," Dunnington said. "I'll check it out this morning."

Morgan nodded at them. "I'll come down to the livery before noon and find out what you learn. Now, I think we better get back to Kristen's house so she can go to work."

"To work?"

"At least you have to stop by and tell your boss you need the day off."

The bank was not open yet when they passed it. They continued on to the general store and found a curious Mrs. Miller.

"Mr. Woo wasn't in his room this morning. What happened to him?"

Morgan told her briefly about their encounter the night before.

"That explains the gunshots and the broken window and the door left open. They must have wanted me to think that Mr. Woo was kidnapped."

She shook her head. "He seemed so sincere in trying to help us figure it out yesterday."

Morgan pointed in back. "I need to look over those plans. That's why the Governor is in town. The whole scheme evidently rides on these plans. I'm beginning to get an idea what it might be about, but I need to check them over again."

"You had breakfast?"

They said they had. Morgan led the way to the first floor living room and took the packet of papers from the back of his shirt. He had thrown away the heavy wrapping and had them tied with a string.

He put them down and read the first page, then nodded.

"Yes, here is a property legal description. A territory must be surveyed, at least with bench marks, before it can be admitted. This first page lists a survey point. Now all I have to do is pick out three or four more and have Carl Dunnington go to the county clerk and find out where they are."

He listed four in the first few pages of the plan, then four more near the end of the more than 100 pages of notes and lines and figures.

Kristen was playing with Lisa. She said she'd go and see the bank manager at her usual time, but she wasn't going to work today.

Morgan learned that Carl Dunnington wasn't at the livery. He went to the county courthouse and found him. Morgan talked with him for a minute, gave him the eight legal descriptions and left.

Morgan again had the engineering plans safely tucked away in his shirt in back. The shirt was full enough so no one could notice. He had just passed the newspaper office when someone called out behind him.

"Mr. Jones. Judson Jones."

For a moment he ignored it, then he remembered. That was the name he had given to Piper Halstead. He turned and saw her standing in a doorway one store back. Morgan walked quickly toward her.

"Good, I caught you," Piper said with a smile. "I wanted to show off our own public library and let you see the progress we're making."

"Well, I'd like to see your library. How many books do you have now?"

"Books? We haven't even counted. We have just

boxes and boxes full that people have given us. Isn't it thrilling?"

Inside the former store, there was general confusion. One bookshelf had been set up on one side, but there was still used lumber, bent nails, sawdust on the floor, no place to put lamps and no tables. No one else was in the old store.

"Looks like you have a way to go," Morgan said.

"True. Could you help me a minute? I need some heavy boxes of books moved so I can start cleaning up the room. They're right over here."

Morgan found a dozen boxes filled with books. He moved them where she had already swept and set them so they could be easily opened.

"Now, what else can I do to help out a worthy cause?" Morgan asked. He delighted in being this close to her. Piper was bright and young and eager and as cute as a newborn fawn. She grinned.

"Well, there is another broom over here."

"Sweeping. That's going to cost you."

She frowned. "Cost me?"

He stepped close to her. "Cost you one kiss."

Her smile faded. "Mr. Jones, that's not at all proper."

"I know, but I couldn't help myself."

Her smile beamed back. "Me either," she said with a husky hint in her voice. She edged closer to him and put her hands on his face. The kiss was short and sweet. She didn't step away but just let go of his face. Her hands fell to his shoulders.

Slowly he bent to kiss her again. She didn't move, just tilted her head up. His arms went around her, and he pulled her against him until her breasts flattened on his chest. The kiss was longer, and she sighed halfway through. He let up just before he felt she would start to struggle.

Gently he let go of her and saw her eyes wide with wonder.

"Mr. Jones! My, that was something, not just a hello-how-are-you kiss."

"That, Piper, was a I-want-to-know-you-better kiss."

"Oh, my goodness. This isn't at all proper."

"I know. Once more?"

She nodded, and he kissed her again, not crushing her so tightly as before but keeping her breasts firmly against his chest and touching her lips with his tongue. When he let her go he could see the stars in her eyes.

"My goodness, Judson. Nobody has ever kissed me that way. I feel all warm and wonderful and kind of confused, and I'm breathing faster than I was. It . . . it feels just marvelous." She shook her head. "But I know I shouldn't. I've talked to other girls. They told me what it was like—I mean the first time. I promised myself it would not happen to me. I'm sorry, but you have to leave now."

"Piper, I didn't mean to go too fast. You're a small, precious jewel. I'd never do anything to hurt you, never, but I will help you sweep. I think I owe you and the library that much help."

"Don't . . . please don't kiss me again. I guess I'm not as strong as I thought I'd be."

"Piper, it's a natural reaction. I had the same feeling. It will happen to you someday, and you'll be ready for it—most likely after you're married. Just remember that it can be the most wonderful experience in your life. Now, where is that broom?"

Chapter Twelve

Morgan swept and helped Piper clean up the old storefront for two hours, then said he had to go talk to someone. Piper came up close to him when he was getting ready to leave.

"Thanks, Judson, I appreciate your help." She grinned. "I also appreciated the kisses." She looked down. "Do you suppose . . ."

"I think it would be all right, Piper, as long as we stay standing up."

She blushed but leaned against him, pressing her breasts against his chest, waiting to be kissed. He held her gently, kissed her once quickly, then again with more insistence. The last time he pressed his tongue against her lips until she opened them and let his tongue drift into her mouth for a moment. When he eased away from her lips she leaned against him, her arms still around him.

"My, my, my," she said, eyes still closed, almost panting for breath. "Oh, my, but that was good. I'd like to order one of those every day." She held up one hand. "But just that much. No more. I think I'd explode if you did that again right now."

"If *we* did that again. You were half of that kiss."

She brightened and pecked a kiss on his cheek. "Glory, I was, wasn't I? I hope you enjoyed it too."

Morgan laughed. "You can be absolutely sure of that. Now I think I better get out of here before I come for another kiss." She waved at him and held a broom in front of her as he walked to the door.

Morgan slipped out to the street and continued toward the Miller General Store. It was past noon. He turned sharply and walked rapidly toward the livery. Dunnington might have found out what they needed to know by now.

He walked into the stable and on to the small office to one side. The owner was there, looking at a map of the territory.

"Hey, Morgan, I was hoping you'd show up. You came up with the damnedest thing. First those plots of land that were bought by both Johnson and Halstead are both on a nearly due north line right out of Denver and on both sides of Lafayette. Beats me what he's up to."

"What about those legal descriptions I gave you?"

Dunnington leaned back and grinned. "This I know for sure you ain't gonna believe."

"Let me guess. The first four are on a compass bearing almost due north out of Denver. The other five are on or near that reverse compass bearing coming south out of Cheyenne."

Dunnington let his hands drop to the desk. "Damn, how did you know that? Took the clerk about half an hour to find all of those legal descriptions on his map. He marked them on this one for us."

"So far the best idea I've come up with is that they had a line surveyed from here to Cheyenne to tie in with the telegraph. That telegraph line would get Denver on the map, make her easy to communicate with from the east or west coast."

"Yes, I see what you mean. But why buy up property? The telegraph people don't buy land to put the poles on; they get some kind of a free pass, a legal easement, to build across anybody's property."

"That's what's bothering me. Maybe it isn't the telegraph. At least we know where it starts and where it goes to. Can I borrow that map?" Morgan asked.

"Sure, I'm not going up there."

Morgan asked for a yardstick and drew a line from the Cheyenne points to those near Denver. "Well, we've got it figured out; we just don't know what 'it' is." He thanked Dunnington, told him to keep his eyes open for some kind of charges they could bring against Johnson, and left by the back alley for the rear of the Miller General Store.

The back door was locked. He knocked three times before she heard him and let him in.

"Good idea keeping this locked," he said.

Mrs. Miller stared at him. "Fritz, the undertaker, was in. Said he hadn't been so busy in weeks. Three bodies this morning and a rumor about three more out of town a ways. Sheriff is going to check on them."

"Boys play with guns, somebody is bound to get hurt. Take a look at this." He showed her the map, explaining the legal descriptions and the points marked. She traced the line with her finger.

"Lord only knows what it could be. A wagon road or maybe a telegraph like you said."

"Then why would Johnson and Halstead be buying up property along the same line?"

Donna Miller snorted. "I'm getting tired of hearing that same question. What we need are some answers. The only place to get them is in that second floor office where Johnson lives."

"Probably true, but there might be one more place. How would you like to go pay the Governor of this fine territory a visit?"

"Me, go see the Governor? How could I do that?"

"Put on your hat and that best dress you've been saving, and you and I will walk right up to that hotel third floor and say howdy. They won't dare do anything to either one of us in broad daylight. Maybe the good Governor will say something he shouldn't.

"All you need are a couple of good complaints to give him. Like we don't have enough territorial law and order out here. Our local sheriff is owned by a local resident, and he won't do anything unless he gets paid for it."

Donna Miller chuckled. "Might be fun at that. I can scream at the Governor and you can get a look around, maybe find or hear something."

A half hour later, they arrived at the hotel and went up to the third floor. There were three people waiting to see the Governor. They sat in a row of chairs outside the great man's door and had to

wait an hour. By the time they got to the door a
young man over six feet tall and built strong and
wide held out his hand for Morgan's weapon.

"No one with a gun gets to see the Governor,"
the man said.

Morgan scowled. "Like me asking you to take
off your pants before you go in that door," Morgan
said. "Look I'm not about to shoot the Governor.
If I was, would I come in here and wait in line
where everyone can see me and identify me? Not
a chance. I'd be outside somewhere with a rifle
and a telescope where nobody could see me."

The door opened to the Governor's room. A man
stood there waiting and frowned at the guard.
"Well?" he said.

Morgan looked at him. The man was Burel
Halstead.

"This man won't give up his side arm, sir."

"So what? He's with Mrs. Miller. I'll vouch for
both of them. The Governor is waiting."

They went inside, and Morgan kept his hand
away from his iron. The Governor sat behind a
desk and nodded at them.

"Governor, we need better law enforcement in
this town," Mrs. Miller said. "Just last night three
men were shot to death on the street and nothing
has been done about it. The problem is the county
sheriff is owned lock, stock and union suit by a
rich man here in town. How long does it take
to get a sheriff recalled? Can you do that by a
governor's decree?"

Morgan looked around the room as Mrs. Miller
stated her case. The Governor replied, but Morgan
didn't hear what he said. There seemed to be nothing in the room that would have anything to do
with the engineering papers. Then Morgan saw a

book that lay on a low table. On the cover of the book was a steam locomotive. The title of the book was *Railroads, the Transportation of the Future*.

Morgan grinned. What else would need a surveyed line. All of those figures could be grade levels! Why didn't he think of it before? The Governor and his cohorts were trying to get a railroad put through. They'd need help from Congress with the land grants, but for that they would need the right of way survey and the grades that would be used for the long, tough haul through the Rocky Mountains.

Morgan wanted to shout out what he had learned, but he forced himself to listen to Mrs. Miller. The Governor shrugged.

"You could hold a recall election, but the man's term runs for only another eight months. Instead you have the right of the ballot to urge every man in the county to vote for a new sheriff. Women are becoming very adept at influencing votes, Mrs. Miller. I strongly suggest that you take that avenue. It will be much more beneficial to the county in the long run."

Morgan nudged her and nodded at the door. "Thank you, Governor. It's good to have you stop by in Lafayette."

They walked out the door, and a man who had been sitting beside them came into the room. He had given up his six-gun, and his empty holster flapped on his thigh.

They hurried out into the sunshine, and Morgan told Mrs. Miller what he had seen in the office and what he suspected.

"That's why they're buying up the land along the right of way. The railroad construction company these men form will have to buy the land to put the rails across it. The individuals can set any price they want to for the land, and the construction company they also own will pay for it from money they get from the government land grants. That's only the start of many ways they can make money off this venture."

"So it is a land grab of sorts," Mrs. Miller said. "How do we stop it?"

"We have it stopped with the engineering right of way and grade level surveys. They must need them in order to go to Congress with a well-researched and organized and already surveyed route. Without that they don't stand a chance to win the contract from the government to build the line."

They walked back to the store. Mrs. Miller unlocked it for two waiting customers and went in. She tended to business while Morgan found some writing paper and pen and ink and began to write a letter.

It was the first step in negotiations.

Morgan had the engineering data.

They needed it to present to Congress.

They would have to pay dearly for it to compensate little Lisa for the death of her mother and probably her grandparents as well.

The note was short and to the point.

"TO: Governor Alonzo Kennedy, Gunther Johnson and Burel Halstead.

I have the engineering report done by Keefe Upton for the right of way and grade levels for the proposed railroad from Denver to Cheyenne. I am keeping it in custody for its legal owner, Lisa Upton, granddaughter of the engineer.

I realize that this is a highly important and valuable document to you. Without it you don't stand a chance of getting congressional approval for the construction of the line and the accompanying land grants under the railroad act.

I alone know where the manuscript is. It is safe, but if any harm comes to Lisa Upton, Mrs. Donna Miller, Kristen Smith or me, you will never see the engineering report, no matter how much money you offer.

Make your first offer by dropping a letter into the regular mail delivery slot in the post office. You have four hours to formulate and send your offer.

Yours faithfully, Lee Morgan."

He read the note again, then let Mrs. Miller read it. She nodded. He sealed it in an envelope and wrote Johnson's name on it then hired a passing young boy for a dime to deliver it to the upstairs office of Gunther Johnson.

Morgan watched the boy until he climbed the stairs. When he came down, Morgan gave him another dime and sauntered back to the general store and post office.

He turned and looked back at the windows of the second story but saw no movement at the curtains. For the first time since he came to this little town, Lee Morgan felt perfectly safe.

He had missed his noon meal and now it was nearing time for the bank to close. He hadn't seen Kristen, but when he went past the financial institution, he saw her at her usual desk. He was on hand when she came out of the building and promptly took her to the best café in town for a steak dinner.

"Celebration?" she asked.

He told her about his guess on the proposed railroad line to Cheyenne, and she laughed and agreed with him.

"Why couldn't we figure it out before?"

They had supper and went back to the general store. The mail slot was on the outside door, with a catch box just inside. He had delivered the note to Johnson at a little after three in the afternoon. By seven that night he was sure there would be a letter in the collection box.

He and Kristen played with Lisa in the apartment.

"Why are you so happy today?" Lisa asked Morgan.

"Because we just learned what your grandpa worked so hard on, and now we know that it's going to mean that you and Mrs. Miller will have all the money you need forever and ever."

Kristen frowned. "How much are you going to ask for?"

"I'm thinking about twenty thousand dollars."

"Oh, so much. A working man earns only about four hundred dollars a whole year. That would be fifty years of wages."

"Which should take Lisa nicely through the most important years of her life."

Lisa looked up from where she was coloring a drawing with crayons. "Are you talking about me?"

"We certainly are, Lisa," Kristen said.

"Why talking?"

"Because you're a fine little girl, and we all love you and want you to grow up to be a fine young lady."

"Like my Mommie?"

"Yes," Morgan said, "just like your mommie."

"Will I be as pretty as she was?"

"Lisa, you're going to be just as pretty as your mother was. I can guarantee it."

Mrs. Miller came in with a stack of letters to send out on the stage the next morning. She riffled through them and dropped one in Morgan's lap.

"Looks like your customers are eager to make an offer."

Morgan tore open the letter and looked at the single sheet of paper.

"The engineering study you refer to is the property of Gunther Johnson, having been contracted for, and the engineer was paid for his services. We will appreciate it being turned over to our representative this evening at eight o'clock at the front door of the Miller General Store.

Upon delivery of the papers, the matter will be considered closed, and no charges of theft or conversion will be lodged with any of the parties mentioned in your letter.

Let's have this done with quickly and get on with our lives."

It was signed by Burel Halstead, attorney for the interests of Gunther Johnson.

Morgan laughed when he had finished reading it. "A lawyer's trick. Ignore the obvious, discount the possible, and go for a complete rout of the strong. It won't work. At eight o'clock I'll deliver them another letter. This one will be worded stronger with references to the State Attorney General's investigation of the deaths of several individuals in town after finding disfavor with Johnson. I'll also include one page of the report, one from the middle of it, and set the price of the remainder at thirty thousand dollars, to be delivered in United States Treasury bank notes within three days."

Kristen rocked Lisa who was getting sleepy. "Will it work?"

"They had to make one bluff. Now that they see it won't work, they'll get down to serious negotiation. I'll ask for an answer from them by nine o'clock at the store's front door."

Mrs. Miller shook her head. "That kind of money is just a dream, a fantasy that I'll never see. I was figuring maybe seven or eight hundred dollars at the most."

"It's no dream, Mrs. Miller. We're in the power position here. We have nothing to lose. They have their multimillion dollar contract to win. They need the right of way and grade level studies to win the right to that contract."

Morgan got busy with his pen and paper again, then went into the back room of the store and returned with page 54 of the engineering study. He put it in an envelope with his demands, double-checked his six-gun and slid in one extra round on the hammer cylinder. He didn't do that often, but it was interesting how many times that sixth round could turn the tide of a fight.

At a quarter to eight, he went into the darkened store and waited. He made the others remain in the apartment. He didn't think there would be any shooting, but who knew?

At five minutes until eight, Morgan saw Halstead walk by. He looked at the dark store and kept going. When he was gone, Morgan lit a lamp and put it on a stool next to the glass door so the light shone outside.

Promptly at eight, Halstead came back, saw the lamp and knocked on the door.

"Mr. Halstead," Morgan said. "Come in. Your legal tricks are unacceptable. Here is my reply. Make certain no one is injured during these negotiations or I'll burn the report and you'll have to start over. That will cost you your support in Congress as well as another year to do the survey. We are demanding thirty thousand dollars for the future support of the child, since Gunther Johnson ordered her mother killed. With that done I won't insist on Johnson being tried for the hired death of Bernice Upton. You know his man killed her. Now get out of here and start raising money, or forget your grand scheme. Oh, all of that land you've been buying up on the proposed right of way will also be little more than worthless if you don't build your railroad."

Halstead began to say something.

"Go, tell the Governor and Johnson to dig into their pockets or the engineering study gets burned to ashes."

Morgan closed and locked the front door as soon as Halstead left. He chuckled at the desperate expression on the lawyer's face. He had only bad news to deliver and that made Morgan a happy man.

He went to the back of the store and found the two women waiting for him. They had heard the exchange.

"So, ladies, how about some whist or even bridge? We have an hour to wait for the Governor's reply."

Chapter Thirteen

Morgan decided not to play cards. He slipped out the front door and walked up the block. The lights were on in the Governor's third floor rooms. He saw figures at the end two windows. Those were the two where they had met the Governor that afternoon.

He wondered if the trio was meeting up there or in Johnson's place. He guessed it would be the fat man's quarters so then the big man wouldn't have to move.

Kristen told Morgan that she had heard that afternoon that the price on his head had been removed. She said the talk was that anyone who harmed Morgan would be run out of town or drawn and quartered, whichever seemed best.

They were getting afraid he might destroy the engineering report. Good.

He walked past the hardware store and looked

up the stairs to the fat man's office.

On a whim he circled around through the alley and watched the rear of the same building. Nothing moved. He saw no lookouts or guards. Evidently the fat man felt secure.

Fine, Morgan decided. Exactly the way he wanted him to feel. If they didn't make a credible response to the offer, Morgan would visit the big man in his own lair late at night.

Morgan relaxed across the street from the hardware and watched the lights over the store. One went out. Another one came on. He checked his watch by the lamp in the saloon next door. It was 8:30. They had a half hour more to reply. He walked down the block and back. Nobody came down the steps.

He hurried back to the general store, but Mrs. Miller said no one had been there. It was after nine. Morgan went inside and decided to take the fight to the enemy. Out in the store, he lit a lamp and began gathering up items that he would need.

He took a half-inch rope, 30 feet long, and a small box of matches, a can of red paint and a small brush. He looked at his supplies and decided they were enough.

"Looks like they aren't going to reply to your last offer," Mrs. Miller said. She had walked up and watched him bundle up the items. He put down two dollars to pay for them, but Mrs. Miller pushed them back in his pocket.

"Going visiting?"

"Aim to later. I figure that Johnson needs a little lesson in how to be polite when you aren't the biggest gun in town."

Morgan played poker with Kristen and Mrs. Miller for two hours using matches for markers.

Kristen won all but a few of the sticks. She was lucky and knew how to play poker.

Morgan checked his watch. "Can Kristen stay here tonight? I'm going to be out for a while. When I get back I'll curl up on the couch."

When Mrs. Miller nodded, he picked up his bag of supplies and went out the alley door. Mrs. Miller locked it behind him.

He spent 15 minutes watching the rear of the Johnson apartment. Nobody moved. There were no guards along the alley, none on either side, and he could spot no one on the roof. He had seen the fire ladder on the back of the building and went up it slowly, checking each rung. At the top he stepped onto the roof of the two story building and moved with cat's feet so he would make no noise. He counted over from the end. He wanted the second window which had been open four inches that afternoon.

He looked over the side of the building but couldn't be sure if it was still open or not. Morgan tied the end of the rope to the two foot false front around the top of the building, then holding the line, he tested it with his weight. It would hold. He let himself over the false front and put his feet on the side of the building.

With his feet anchored and his hands gripping the rope, he could walk down the side of the building with ease. He came down between two dark windows. The second one on his left was still open four inches. He held himself with one hand and pushed upward on the window. It rose with ease without scraping.

Morgan turned and slid in through the open window, then got his feet on the floor and let go of the rope. He looked around in the faint light and saw it was an office. Quietly he scattered papers, dumped out files on the floor and overturned chairs, but all without any noise.

He tested the door. Unlocked. Morgan moved down the hall to the next door and tried it. The door came open. Another office. He scattered files again and dumped out drawers, and when he felt satisfied, he opened the can of paint and printed on the wall.

"Morgan was here."

He went to the next room and was about to try the handle when someone walked out of the room. The man stared at Morgan for just a moment, then Morgan smashed his hard fist into the surprised man's jaw. His head snapped to one side, and he blasted back into the room and sprawled on the floor unconscious.

Morgan grinned, tied up the man and gagged him, then looked around the room. It had two bunks on one side and a closet. A barracks for Johnson's guards. They weren't doing much of a job for him.

He went back into the hallway and printed on the long wall the same message. "Morgan was here. Johnson: You would be dead by now if I wanted you dead."

Morgan decided he had made his point. Morgan walked across the hall and looked at Halstead's office but shook his head and went down the steps silently to the street, hurrying back to the general store.

Mrs. Miller waited for him at the front door and let him in.

"A reply came to the box about ten minutes after you left," she said. "I almost read it, but I decided to wait."

Morgan took the letter and tore it open. At the counter in back, Mrs. Miller set down the lamp and turned up the wick. Morgan read the message out loud.

"Morgan. You have the goods we want. We agree to pay you $5,000 for the complete return and your total silence on this and any other happening in the Territory of Colorado. If such a settlement is agreed to, we will make arrangements in the morning. Someone will be at this door at 8 A.M."

Morgan grinned in the lamplight.

"We've got them. Once they get the idea they have to pay we'll start the negotiating. They'll come up from five, and I'll come down from thirty. I'd say we'll get the twenty thousand I figured on all the time."

Mrs. Miller smiled. "I never thought that you'd win against Johnson and Halstead. Glad you did. The whole town will thank you." She paused. "You have a minute? I need to tell you something. Down this way." She led him to the apartment and indicated Lisa's room.

"Little darling is sleeping soundly. I'm lucky to have her. Kristen is asleep upstairs. Come in here."

Morgan stepped into the room and by the thin lamp light saw it was a bedroom.

"Morgan, I've taken Lisa off your hands. I've covered for you and put up with you. What have I asked for in return for all of this kindness?"

"Not a thing, Mrs. Miller. You're a saint."

"A saint I'm not. What I am is hungry. Morgan, I've been a widow for three years. Haven't even seen a man's bare chest in that time let alone the good parts. I want you tonight, Morgan, all naked and hard and willing and in my bed until dawn.

Hell, you don't even have to look at me. I sag in places and bulge in other places. I'm forty-four years old, but I still feel sexy as hell sometimes. We'll turn the lights off, that is after I get my fill of looking at your beautiful, hard, naked, male body. Do I offend you?"

"Not a bit, Donna. Some widows don't need sex any more, some do. He moved in front of her and touched her breasts. "Do you want to undress me?"

"Oh, God, yes!"

She brought in another lamp and then took off his clothes slowly, loving every minute of it. She rubbed his hard chest and flat belly, marveling at them.

When she came to his underwear she hesitated. "Damn, I'm nervous! Can you fancy that? I'm like a virgin bride on her wedding night."

She still had on all her clothes. She stripped his shorts down quickly. His erection caught on the fabric, and she grunted in surprise.

"Oh, damn, look at him, so eager to meet my old pussy!" She blew out one light and turned and undressed. Morgan smiled as he watched her. She was as nervous as a bride all right. She turned around and hesitated.

She was thick-waisted, with heavy breasts sagging a bit. Her thighs were large but solid, and her legs tapered quickly to fine ankles.

"So, shall I turn out the lights and put a sack over my head."

"Not a chance," Morgan said. He rolled over on the bed, leaving room for her. Now she gained confidence, dropped on the quilt beside him and at once grabbed his erection.

"You know how long it's been, Morgan? Three

years. I ain't even seen a cock in three long lonely years."

"You should take a lover and then marry him, Donna. More important now. Little Lisa needs a father around the place."

"Damned if I ain't gonna do it. I had a couple of chances. Mostly they wanted the store. But hell, that's a bargaining chip for me now. God, Morgan throw that pole into me. I don't need none of that foreplay."

It was the wildest, strangest night that Morgan could remember. She taught Morgan a position or two that he hadn't even thought of.

"Older you get the more you try to find something new," she told him as they rested between times. She went and found cheese and crackers and some fresh apples and then brought in a bottle of white wine.

"For emergencies," she said. "Hell, don't know when I'll have another emergency like this one."

They both laughed. Morgan pulled the cork, and they sampled the wine. It was better than any Morgan had tasted in a long time.

"My former husband was the wine expert. He sent to New York to get it. Came from France, I think."

By midnight Donna was getting tired. "Once more and then I gotta get some sleep. Some of us have to put in a full twelve hour day at the store tomorrow. You ever do the Manchurian pretzel?"

Morgan laughed and said he hadn't.

"Neither have I. One more regular and I'll be sore for a week, but it's been too damn long since I been pussy sore."

*   *   *

The next morning, Morgan woke up at six A.M. as usual. He dressed and went into the kitchen. By the time Mrs. Miller came out he had sliced fried potatoes and onions ready and then fried two eggs sunny side up and served her at the kitchen table.

"Hey, Morgan, you eligible for staying on here as cook and bed partner?"

"Afraid not. I had a job in Omaha if it's still there."

"Damn, too much to expect. Not many men I know can even boil water."

Kristen came down looking tousled and delicious, but Morgan looked away. She grinned and in a second figured out what had happened last night just by looking at Mrs. Miller.

"You two were kind of wild last night and noisy, but I must say you only woke me up once. At first I thought we were being attacked by a band of Cheyenne."

Mrs. Miller laughed until she brushed tears out of her eyes.

"Girl, you should know how good this man is. Had to take my try at him before he got away."

"Good for you," Kristen said, and the two women exchanged secret women looks and Morgan had no idea what they meant.

By eight o'clock, the store was open, and five minutes later Burel Halstead came in the front door with a slender leather case he held on to tightly. He approached Morgan, and his face was grim.

"I take it we have an agreement on the figure discussed in the letter," he said.

"Not a chance," Morgan said. "Let's take a walk and do some talking. We're going to negotiate. Ordinarily I don't talk with killers, but in this case a small girl's future is at stake. After you, Mr. Halstead."

They went to the boardwalk and turned north.

"See here, Morgan, this is outrageous. The engineering work was done and paid for. Upton never delivered. Legally it belongs to Mr. Johnson. Any court in the territory would award it to him."

"Any court outside of Lafayette would also charge both you and Johnson with murder in the death of Bernice Upton. If you want to go to court, I'll be glad to testify. Johnson will hang for sure; you'll probably get off with ten years in the territorial prison."

"Now see here. I don't need a lecture on the law."

"You need lots of lectures. I said thirty thousand in my offer. I'll cut that down to twenty-seven thousand five hundred. I've got to think of the little girl's future."

"Ten thousand, our top offer."

"That railroad contract is worth nearly a hundred million dollars. You'll get twenty sections of land for every mile of track you complete. It's rugged mountain territory. The timber rights alone will be worth a hundred million dollars within ten years. Now you're haggling about a few thousand dollars." He hesitated. "All right, I'll come down to twenty-five thousand."

Halstead's grim face hardened. "It's going to cost a million dollars a mile to build some of those stretches. We'll be lucky to come out with a million dollars profit." He shrugged. I'm authorized to go to fifteen thousand dollars."

They had walked to the edge of town. Morgan laughed softly and they turned and headed back. By the time they reached the general store, the two men had agreed on $22,500. The cash would be brought from Denver the following day. He had $5,000 in cash in the briefcase that would serve as a down payment.

"You'll get the engineering report when we have all of the cash," Morgan said.

"We need more security. For the five thousand we require the first five pages of the study and the last five. Is that agreeable?"

Morgan thought it over. Reasonable. Yes. "I'll need the rest of the day to get those pages for you. You didn't think I carried them around in my pocket, did you?"

"Shall we say at eight o'clock tonight at the general store's front door."

"Done. I'll be here."

When Halstead walked away, Morgan saw that he was smiling. He still had the five thousand and the promise of ten pages of the study. Morgan guessed he was smiling for an entirely different reason.

Five minutes later, Morgan headed for the livery. He told the women how he came out on the negotiations. "Now I have to ride somewhere and pretend to find the documents. That's when they'll jump me. The good part is I get to pick the place so I'll have the terrain advantage."

"They'll try to kill you and then take the document," Kristen said.

"True, but they've tried before."

At the front door just before he left, Morgan told Mrs. Miller where the engineering study was hidden in the back room of the store on the chance he didn't come back.

She shushed him. "No man alive can kill you, Morgan. The women of the world would rise up and smash them if they tried. Now get those slender hips and that great body out of here."

At the stable, he told Dunnington what he was doing. The livery man gave him a Spencer rifle he'd used before and three extra tubes loaded with seven rounds each of the .52 caliber shells.

"You know the land, Dunnington. I want a spot where I can have terrain advantage. Where should I go within an hour or two?"

The livery man told him, and Morgan rode out. Only once in the first hour did he detect the men behind him. On a long open stretch he saw three riders crest the small hill behind him, then vanish almost at once. At least three. He figured more like ten. Johnson wouldn't want to leave this to chance. He had a way to get the document without paying a dime. He'd hire 20 men if he thought it would help.

Morgan found the spot Dunnington told him about a half hour later. It was across a small stream that had dug a canyon 40 feet deep. There was no way for a horse to get across the gully and up the other side. It was a scramble to make it on foot.

Morgan fell once and rolled down ten feet before he caught himself. Then he worked slower and held the Spencer out of the dirt as he got up the shelves and ledges to the top. There was a jumble of rocks there from an old rock fall that made a perfect fort. He slid in behind them and saw that there were holes between some large boulders that gave him perfect firing lines into the opposite bank and for a quarter of a mile beyond. There was little cover here—nothing to hide a horse.

Any attack would have to be made across a quarter mile of open land, then down the gully on one side and up it on the other side. Morgan nodded and settled in to wait.

He saw the first man run from one scrub tree to another about 20 minutes later. Morgan's horse was tied to a tree on the far side of the ravine.

The killers must figure he was still there getting the papers. Fifteen minutes later he saw that ten men had moved across the flat space. Half of them were at the edge of the ravine.

Morgan found a good opening and bellowed to the men no more than 40 yards away.

"You men hired by Johnson. This isn't your fight. You stay here you're dead men. You have five minutes to turn around and get out of here." When he finished the offer he sent two rifle rounds into a stub tree near where two men lay behind rocks.

One man pushed back from the ravine, turned and ran downstream. Someone fired a rifle at the man, but he got away.

"Come and get me!" Morgan bellowed. Then he sighted in on the closest man to the ravine. The Spencer spoke, and the hired gun kneeling behind a small bush screamed in pain then pitched sideways and didn't move.

Morgan turned to a new target. It was going to be a long afternoon.

Chapter Fourteen

Morgan wasn't trying to kill the men who were try-ing to kill him. He consciously aimed at their legs despite knowing they were a smaller target, but he had all the advantages. One man made it over the edge of the ravine and slid down the side.

Morgan nailed him to the wall with a chest shot, and he died with a series of wild, agonizing screams. After that no one tried to get across the gully.

He shot four more of them, three in the legs and one in the shoulder. He tried to pick out the leader of the group but couldn't. He fired twice at the last man in the formation but missed.

Morgan reloaded the tubes once, and then saw the first man turn and run back to his horse. After that it was only a matter of time. He shot two more attackers in the legs, and they hobbled away. They were easy targets, but he let them go.

Two men lay dead in or near the ravine when the last man got up and ran to the rear in a zigzag pattern that would make it almost impossible to hit him.

Morgan watched the last man mount up a quarter of a mile away and ride toward Lafayette.

Through it all his horse had remained tied to the same small tree. He thought maybe one of the men would kill the animal, and he was prepared to walk back to town. Now he wouldn't have to.

He left his fortress, worked down the bank and up the other side. He picked a roundabout way to ride back to Lafayette, so he wouldn't come on any stragglers from the fight. What could he say to a man he had shot?

Morgan got back to town about four that afternoon. He was starved and remembered he didn't have any noon meal. He stopped at a café and ate a steak, then went to the general store. Mrs. Miller hugged him, Kristen kissed him, and Morgan felt better at once.

After the store closed, the three sat around the kitchen table sipping coffee.

"I wouldn't know what to do with all that money if we ever get it," Mrs. Miller said.

"I'd get it all in gold and keep it in a trunk in my room," Kristen said. "I'm not too wild about trusting banks."

Morgan chuckled. "A man in Chicago told me if I ever got money to use it in several ways and spread it around. He said put one-third of it into real estate. Buy a couple of stores here in town say. A third of it should go into good quality stocks where your money can earn dividends for you and the stock might go up in value. Then a third of it should be kept available, such as in a bank savings account, probably in the biggest bank in Denver."

"I'll think on it," Mrs. Miller said.

Morgan scowled at his coffee cup. "I still don't like the idea of Johnson getting off free and clear on all this. He ordered Bernice Upton killed. I know that for fact."

"An eye for an eye," Kristen said.

"I'm not the jury or the executioner," Morgan said. "Still it sticks in my craw that he killed more than one man and now he's going to get that railroad contract and wind up filthy rich."

"You could always do something about it," Mrs. Miller said. "The town would be happy. We'll get a new sheriff come election time and he won't be owned by nobody."

"The Governor went back to Denver this afternoon," Kristen said. "I saw his big coach pull out with its six blacks. Impressive."

"I hope he has the money ready," Morgan said.

"You've never met our Gunther Johnson, have you, Morgan?" Mrs. Miller asked.

"Never had the pleasure."

"I think you should tonight. Meet him, talk with him and let nature take its course."

"Meaning I'll get so furious with him I'll kill the man?"

"Probably, Morgan, and it would be a miracle from heaven if you did."

"I might just pay him a visit. I should know the men I'm doing business with."

Morgan left the store at midnight. Only the saloons were open, and two were full and erupting now and then with small fights that moved out to the street. Morgan picked his way through them and went up the stairway to the fat man's quarters. He used two small steel tools and quickly opened the lock on the door with the Johnson name.

He stepped into the room quietly. It was dark. There was a sliver of light coming from under a far door.

Morgan moved silently to the door and tested the knob. It turned without sound, and he eased the door forward an inch. He could see little through the slit. He listened.

Nothing.

Morgan slid the door open another inch. He had his Colt up and ready as he pushed the door wide open. It led into the hallway. He had forgotten. He looked in the rooms he hadn't been in the night before. One of them must be Johnson's bedroom. He found it behind the third door he tried. It was unlocked.

Morgan had seen no one else in the offices and apartment.

The bedroom had been made by taking out one of the walls. It was huge, and a large, heavily reinforced bed sat against the far wall. The huge chair with wheels stood beside the bed, and Johnson lay in the chair sleeping.

Maybe he was too tired to get into bed.

Morgan left the room and checked the rest of the rooms on the second floor. There were no guards. He opened one and saw that it led to the ramp from the second floor to the ground in the alley.

Back in Johnson's bedroom, Morgan slapped the man hard across the face.

He woke up with a bellow of anger. The first thing he saw was the muzzle of Morgan's .45 three inches from his eyes.

"What in hell?"

"No, Mr. Johnson, not hell quite yet. That won't come for you for several hours yet, depending on how well you cooperate. My name is Lee Morgan. I don't think we've met. I didn't see you when I was here last night. Your painters did a good job covering up my work.

"What the hell do you want?"

"Besides the twenty-two thousand five hundred dollars? Besides that I want some justice. How many men have you had killed since you've been in power here, Johnson?"

"I don't know what you mean."

"Murder—you know damn well what I mean. People around town can count up at least ten men who you have had killed. You know you're just as guilty of murder if you hire it to be done as if you pull the trigger."

"My lawyer—"

"Your lawyer isn't here, so you must give your own defense. You see, Johnson, you're on trial for your life, before me, your prosecutor, your judge, your jury—and in case you're guilty, I'm also your executioner.

"Now what kind of a defense do you have?"

Morgan hoped it would be easy, but the man was so heavy that even his hands moved slowly. By the time he had the twin barrel derringer out of its hiding place and started to swing it upward, Morgan had slashed hard down on his wrist with the heavy Colt.

Morgan heard the wrist bone snap, and Johnson gasped with pain.

The one man court took the derringer and felt around the chair for more weapons. He found a throwing knife, a stiletto and another derringer, this one a small one shot .22 caliber.

"Now, let's get down to cases. You hired Brice O'Gallon to take care of Bernice Upton. He was also supposed to get the engineering report back from her. He completed only half of his task. How do you plead on the charge of murdering Bernice Upton?"

"Go to hell, Morgan."

"That's your next ticket, fat man, not mine. No defense. The prosecution has seen the lady die, has heard her lips describe the killer, and has testimony that the killer worked on specific instructions from you.

"The judge finds you guilty of murder and sentences you to hang. So, the next step is to take you to jail. I'm sure the sheriff will have room. Probably have to build a new heavier gallows and use a cable instead of rope, but we'll manage."

Morgan moved to the back of the chair, studied it a moment, then pulled back a braking device that pressed against the wheels and turned the big chair.

"Where the hell we going?"

"To jail, as I told you. I'll let the county hang you. I don't have the proper credentials for that. I'd end up strangling you instead of a clean break of your neck."

"Hell you say. Go get Doc Gilroy. He's got to set my wrist. You broke it, you bastard."

"You had me worried for a while. Your plans for the railroad are legal. Your bribing of Congress may not be, but everyone does it. I was afraid you might get away with it, but then the murder case came up. You can't run away from murder."

"What about the men you've killed here in town,

Morgan? I know at least six of my men you've killed."

"Correct, but they were all in self-defense. Those were the men you sent to kill me, so they too are six more murders charged against you. Shall we have a trial on each of those men, too?"

"Stop! Don't move me. You don't know how."

"How? Just move you back to the ramp and take you down to the ground, easy."

"No, no. It takes four strong men to take me down there."

"We'll see."

"No!"

Morgan ignored the pleas and rolled the big man through the double door and down the hall toward the ramp. He had no idea how to get the heavy chair and heavy body down the ramp. He would worry about that when the time came.

"You can't do this. It's murder. Money. Yeah, cash. Stop right here and I'll give you all the cash I have in my safe."

Morgan stopped the chair. "How much?"

"I've got that five thousand, plus another two or three thousand."

"Let's go get it."

Morgan turned the chair and wheeled him back to his main office where Johnson moved a panel from the wall and dialed a combination on a wall safe. He turned the handle and was about to reach in when Morgan stopped him. He pushed the chair back and opened the foot wide door. Inside was a foot square, solid metal safe.

Right on top lay a six-gun loaded and cocked. Morgan pushed it to one side and took out stacks of U.S. bank notes. He pushed them inside his shirt.

"Is this all the cash you've got?"

"That's it. Now wheel me back to my bedroom and you can leave."

"Hey, we're friends now. I can't desert you. Let me take you for a walk."

Morgan wheeled him back down the hall to the double doors that opened on the ramp.

"Hey, you said you'd take the money."

"True, but I didn't say that I'd let you live. Your time is up, big man. You're ready to move on into the next world—whatever that's going to be for you."

Morgan opened the doors and pushed the chair out. There was a flat place, then a gradual ramp that increased in slope until it reached the ground.

Johnson turned to Morgan. The large man's face was red, and his eyes shot fire as he glared at Morgan.

"Damnit, that's enough! Roll me back in. You can't do this."

"Do what? Your chair is balanced. As long as you stay entirely still it won't move. Of course, Gunther old man, if you wiggle or try to move or even reach for the hand brake, it will be enough for you to start moving forward. You might roll all the way to the bottom, and then again you might crash off the side of the ramp and drop down there about twenty feet.

"I'll just move on back down the hall so I don't upset you any. I'd just hate to be the cause of your rolling down there and smashing your body into five hundred pounds of bloody pulp."

Morgan stepped behind the man where Johnson couldn't see him. He stopped and watched.

"Help!" Johnson called.

"Help. I'm up here on the second floor." He

screamed it this time, but nobody came to help
him. It was well after midnight and there were
no back doors to saloons around his building.

"Damnit, this can't be happening. I planned
everything too well. It can't go this wrong."

Morgan leaned against the wall. He watched
the chair move slightly. The heavy man must be
reaching for the hand brake.

Johnson yelped as the chair moved forward an
inch. He surged from one side to lunge for the hand
brake. That motion nudged the rig forward again,
and suddenly it was rolling straight down the ramp.

Johnson screamed. The chair rolled faster and
faster until it hit the sharp upward angle of the
ground at the bottom of the ramp. Morgan had
watched the chair roll all the way down. The
chair's small wheels hit the sharp slope of the
alley and almost stopped.

Johnson catapulted off the chair and turned half
over before he smashed into the hard dirt of the
alley. A fraction of a second later the heavy chair
bounced into the air and came crashing down on
top of the bloated body.

Morgan waited a moment more, but heard nothing from below—no cries for help, no weeping,
no death cry. Morgan left the ramp doors open
and walked down the hall to the front door. He
went out and down to the street. When no one
was looking, he stepped out of the stairs to the
boardwalk and hurried toward the general store.

He had to knock three times on the back door
before Mrs. Miller came to let him in.

He took her into the kitchen where she lit a
lamp. He pulled the stacks of bills from his shirt
and set them on the table. He divided them into
two stacks.

One of them he put his hands on. "Mr. Johnson won't be needing this any more. He gave it to me. This half is my fee for cleaning up the garbage in this town. The rest of it is for you and Lisa."

"He's dead?"

"Had a terrible accident down the ramp on his chair. I have no idea where he was going."

Mrs. Johnson smiled and swept the money into a drawer in the kitchen. "Tomorrow we'll talk," she said.

The next morning at eight o'clock Burel Halstead came to the front of the store and waited for Morgan.

"You must have heard about the accident last night."

Morgan shook his head. "I just got up."

"Mr. Johnson evidently rolled down the ramp from his second floor apartment, crashed at the bottom and was fatally injured."

"Oh, the death of any human being is always a tragedy."

"This will make no difference in our arrangements," Halstead went on quickly. "We won't need the partial now. We'll have the agreed upon amount of cash for you this afternoon here at the store, and we hope that you'll have the documents here."

"They will be, Mr. Halstead. I don't know how tightly you were tied in with Mr. Johnson and his murderous rampages. You might be as guilty as he is. The only reason I'm not going to prosecute you is your lovely young daughter. My advice to you is to pay more attention to her. Help her get her library set up and operating, and tread the straight and narrow on this railroad construction company, keeping it a strictly honest venture with the Governor."

"Mr. Morgan, we have underestimated you. Indeed I am not totally blameless, but I ordered no one killed. I will do my best to keep the railroad project on the legal, moral and ethical path."

Three days later everything settled down. Morgan and Mrs. Miller had taken, $20,000 of the money to the Colorado Bank in Denver and deposited it. It was the strongest and best financed bank in the state. The other $2,500 she put in a special bank account there in Lafayette which would be used only for Lisa's welfare. They split the $7,500 from Johnson's safe. Morgan put most of his in the Denver bank as well.

Kristen was back at the bank working hard on the accounts. That night she rolled over in bed in her house and looked up at Morgan.

"Strange, isn't it, how people meet and have an affect on each other, and then in just a few days those two persons part probably never to meet again."

"Strange, yes, but not unusual. You said a gentleman friend of yours was coming back to town?"

"Yes. He was real sweet on me last year, then he had to go to Denver for a while. Oh, we kissed and hugged a little but we never, you know, were in bed. I thought he was just about ready to ask me to marry him. Now we'll have to start all over."

"Take it easy, girl. Don't rush him. Then if he hasn't asked you to marry him in three months, invite him over here for dinner and then spill something on yourself and ask him to help you take off your dress. If that doesn't do it, dump the no-account and find a new man."

He bent and kissed her breasts.

"Now, once more for good luck, then we need some sleep."

The next morning, Morgan had brought his horse from the livery and was at the front of the Miller General Store. He held Lisa, and she threw her arms around him and kissed his cheek.

"Thank you for finding me a new mommie," Lisa said.

Mrs. Miller blinked tears out of her eyes.

A young woman came rushing down the board-walk. She hurried up to Morgan just as he handed Lisa to Mrs. Miller.

"There you are," Piper Halstead said. "I was afraid I was going to miss you." She caught his hand. "Let's walk up the street a ways."

As they walked she talked. "I knew you weren't Judson that first day, but I didn't know your name. Then I saw you talking with Daddy. Thank you for not getting him mixed up in the terrible things that Mr. Johnson did. Also I thank you for giving me my first real kiss. One more?"

She reached up and kissed his lips gently. "I'll always remember you, Lee Morgan. Next time you're through here you stop by and see me." She turned and walked away up the street leaving him with a small smile over her shoulder.

Morgan mounted his horse and waved good-bye to Lisa and Mrs. Miller. With any luck at all he might make Denver tonight and a good night's sleep before he headed out on the stage for Cheyenne. There was a chance that job back east was still open.

KIT DALTON

GIANT SPECIAL EDITIONS

More girls...more guns...more rip-roarin' adventure — in one low-priced volume!

NIGHT RIDER'S MOON. When Buckskin Lee Morgan headed out to Miles City, Montana, to help a friend in distress, he soon found troubles of his own. For an old warrant was still out on him, and more than one bounty hunter wanted to exchange his corpse for a pile of gold.
_3056-X $3.95

BOUNTY HUNTER'S MOON. Morgan headed for Rawlings, Wyoming, to find the kidnapped daughter of a powerful brewery owner, but he didn't count on being sidetracked along the way by some vicious bounty hunters and a bevy of bank-robbing beauties.
_2777-1 $3.95

THE BUCKSKIN BREED. Morgan's father had given him the determination to use a gun, but he hadn't told Morgan about the passel of other children he had sired. Now, he found himself fighting his own brother, and only the winner would walk away with his life.
_2587-6 $3.95

LEISURE BOOKS
ATTN: Order Department
276 5th Avenue, New York, NY 10001

Please add $1.50 for shipping and handling for the first book and $.35 for each book thereafter. N.Y.S. and N.Y.C. residents, please add appropriate sales tax. No cash, stamps, or C.O.D.s. All orders shipped within 6 weeks via postal service book rate. Canadian orders require $2.00 extra postage. It must also be paid in U.S. dollars through a U.S. banking facility.

Name _____
Address _____
City _____ State _____ Zip _____
I have enclosed $_____in payment for the checked book(s).
Payment <u>must</u> accompany all orders.☐ Please send a free catalog.

2β5 JW